KT-442-460

She looked at Jason, who was teaching Tommy how to cut out paper Santas, and her heart swelled with love.

Her son was so happy, so relaxed, and she knew a lot of it was to do with the easy acceptance given by Jason. Jason—who had not only accepted Tommy but had accepted her as well.

Easy acceptance. The people here, those she worked with, liked her for who she was—not for her family name. She was simply Summer, and it had been far too long since she'd felt that way.

Jason had figured it out, though. He knew of the Hoyts family, knew of their influence, and yet it hadn't fazed him one bit. He was caring and sincere. Helpful and honest. It was no wonder she was falling in love with him. It also helped that he was drop-dead sexy. She smiled to herself, acknowledging the extent of her feelings for him. For some reason it didn't bother her. She was falling in love, and although it was terrifying it was addictively exhilarating at the same time. And it made her feel…truly alive.

Lucy Clark is a husband-and-wife writing team. They enjoy taking holidays with their children, during which they discuss and develop new ideas for their books using the fantastic Australian scenery. They use their daily walks to talk over characterisation and fine details of the wonderful stories they produce, and are avid movie buffs. They live on the edge of a popular wine district in South Australia, with their two children, and enjoy spending family time together at weekends.

Recent titles by the same author:

CITY SURGEON, OUTBACK BRIDE
A WEDDING AT LIMESTONE COAST
HER VERY SPECIAL BABY
HIS CHRISTMAS PROPOSAL

CHILDREN'S DOCTOR, CHRISTMAS BRIDE

BY
LUCY CLARK

MILLS & BOON®

Pure reading pleasure™

All the characters in this book have no existence outside
the imagination of the author, and have no relation
whatsoever to anyone bearing the same name or names.
They are not even distantly inspired by any individual
known or unknown to the author, and all the incidents
are pure invention.

All Rights Reserved including the right of reproduction
in whole or in part in any form. This edition is published
by arrangement with Harlequin Enterprises II BV/S.à.r.l.
The text of this publication or any part thereof may
not be reproduced or transmitted in any form or by
any means, electronic or mechanical, including
photocopying, recording, storage in an information
retrieval system, or otherwise, without the written
permission of the publisher.

® and TM are trademarks owned and used by the
trademark owner and/or its licensee. Trademarks marked
with ® are registered with the United Kingdom Patent
Office and/or the Office for Harmonisation in the
Internal Market and in other countries.

First published in Great Britain 2008
Large Print edition 2009
Harlequin Mills & Boon Limited,
Eton House, 18-24 Paradise Road,
Richmond, Surrey TW9 1SR

© Anne Clark and Peter Clark 2008

ISBN: 978 0 263 20518 3

Set in Times Roman 16¾ on 19¼ pt.
17-0609-50754

Printed and bound in Great Britain
by CPI Antony Rowe, Chippenham, Wiltshire

CHILDREN'S DOCTOR, CHRISTMAS BRIDE

To Dustin. Welcome to the family!
Psalm 111:1

CHAPTER ONE

SUMMER HOYTS held her son's hand as they made their way through the crowded, open-air shopping mall. The cool breeze certainly helped, given the amount of people who had turned out on a Saturday evening to see the enormous Christmas tree positioned in the centre of the complex.

This would be their first Christmas in Ballarat. Their first Christmas away from the pressures of their old life in Sydney. Had she done the right thing? Not for the first time since they'd boarded the plane two days ago and arrived in their new town, Summer had a twinge of apprehension. She'd uprooted both herself and her son from the pretentious life they'd been forced to live in Sydney.

Shaking her head to clear her thoughts, she told herself she'd done the right thing. She'd been given full custody of her son and it was now time to make a new life for themselves, away from her power-hungry in-laws. A job had been going in Ballarat for a new paediatrician and she'd jumped at the chance.

Her seven-year-old son, Tommy, had lived all his life in their large inner-city penthouse in a prominent part of Sydney's social society and now they were here, in rural Ballarat. It was certainly a change but she hoped, given his age, it wouldn't take him too long to adapt to a different style of life.

'Mum?' Tommy tugged on her hand. 'I'm thirsty. May I have my drink, please?'

'Just give me a second to find somewhere to sit. I didn't expect there to be so many people.'

It didn't matter whether other people thought she'd done the right thing or not—the fact was, she'd done it. Against the advice of her friends—or those that she'd called her friends for the past ten years—she'd made the move and today she was determined to bring a little bit of Christmas cheer into their lives by attending the town's first Christmas event—the lighting-up of the large artificial Christmas tree.

'We'll try over there.' She pointed so Tommy would know in which direction she wanted to head. 'I think I saw an empty bench seat.'

'It'll be taken. We should have got here earlier. If we were in Sydney, we would have sent the maid to reserve our seat hours ago.'

'We don't have maids any more, Tommy,' she reminded him gently, trying to ignore the hint of bitterness in his voice. He hadn't wanted to leave Sydney but that was because he hadn't ever known anything different.

Summer held his hand firmly and continued to head through the crowd, trying to avoid crying toddlers, mothers with strollers and the rest of the shoppers who were out to enjoy the festivities. To be honest, she hadn't expected so many people to be here. This was a small town, not a big city! As they drew closer to the bench she realised someone was already sitting there.

A man, who she judged to be in his late thirties, was leaning forward to talk to a child in a wheelchair which was parked beside the bench. He pointed up at something and the child slowly turned his head and looked. The patch on the boy's eye made Summer realise he'd not long ago had eye surgery.

She stopped and watched as a smile crossed the boy's face. The man was smiling, too, and Summer's breath caught in her throat at the sight. He had dark brown hair, twinkling brown eyes and a smile which made her heart skip a beat. She closed her eyes for a second, getting her mind back on track. She hadn't come here to ogle strange men.

She gave Tommy's hand a little squeeze as she once more scanned the crowd to try to find a place where they could watch the event.

'Are you looking for someone?'

Summer turned her head at the deep, rich voice and knew it belonged to the stranger. 'Sorry?' She met his eyes and realised that they weren't just a run-of-the-mill, everyday brown. Instead they were flecked with yellow and gold as well and radiated warmth and friendliness.

'Are you looking for someone?' He repeated his question.

'No. I'm trying to find somewhere my son and I can sit.'

He shifted along to the end of the bench. 'You can sit here. There's plenty of room.'

Wariness prickled along the back of her neck. Should she accept? As she looked around at the crowds, she realised if they wanted to get a decent view, she really had no option. 'Oh. Uh…thank you.' Summer headed closer and let go of Tommy's hand as he sat down. 'That's very kind.' Polite. All she had to be was polite.

'You're welcome.' He stuck out his hand. 'I'm Jason Daniels.'

'Summer Hoyts.' His handshake was firm and she appreciated that, although his grasp seemed to linger a little longer than was usually polite. Then again, perhaps that was just one of those differences between big city and country town. She forced a smile as she let go. 'This is my son, Tommy.'

'Hi.' He gave Jason a brief wave. 'Mum! Water? Please?'

'I know.' She quickly took the backpack from her shoulders, pulled out a water bottle and handed it to her son.

'Thanks, Mum,' he said, before taking a drink.

'It's a hotter day than usual for October,' Jason

said conversationally as he swatted at a fly. He turned to look at the boy in the wheelchair, making sure the boy's hat was on tight. 'You all right, Bradley?'

'Yep. JD? When are the others getting here?'

'Soon. They left after us, remember. At least we have priority parking.'

'Others?' Summer asked, surprised the boy hadn't called him 'Dad'. 'Will there be enough room for them?'

Jason immediately waved away her concern. 'Of course. There aren't that many. Three more children and two more adults. We can all squish onto the bench together.' He glanced over his shoulder and then waved at someone in the crowd. 'And here they are.'

Summer turned and looked in the same direction. There were two women in nursing uniforms heading towards them. One was pushing a child in a wheelchair whose legs were secured in a hip spica cast, and the other had a toddler on her hip and was holding the hand of a little girl.

'They're from the hospital!' Summer was surprised.

'We thought we'd give them a bit of respite

from the four walls they've been confined to. Especially the twins.'

'You're a doctor?'

'I am.' As his friends came over, Jason introduced them. 'Summer, I'd like you to meet Alyssa and Rhonda—two of my fellow colleagues—and this is Katy…' He pointed to the toddler in Rhonda's arms and then to the identical twin girls. 'And Sally and Sasha.'

'Hello.' Summer smiled at the girls. Sasha was the girl in the wheelchair, her legs secured in a pink cast with a metal bar between the legs to ensure her bones would heal in the correct position. Little Katy had a bandage around her head, covering one ear. As far as Summer could see, there didn't seem to be anything wrong with Sally but, then, that was only from outward appearances.

She bent down so she could talk to Sasha after the wheelchair had been parked at the other end of the bench. 'Glad to be outside?' she asked the child.

'Oh, yes,' she said with a very firm nod, her eyes wide with excitement. Sally came over and leant on the wheelchair next to her sister.

'Sashy broke her legs.'

'I can see that. It must have hurt.'

'It did. I was berry brave. I only cried a bit.'

'That's true,' Jason interjected as he came over to them. Rhonda and Alyssa were settling Katy and checking on Bradley. 'When the ambulance arrived at the hospital, Sasha was the bravest four-year-old I've seen in ages.'

'*I* didn't get hurt, did I, Dr JD?' Sally said. 'But I was really sad for my twinny.'

'I'm glad you didn't get hurt, too,' Summer agreed, but also couldn't help noticing the admission band on Sally's wrist. 'Did you get a wristband like your sister?'

'I'm staying at the hopsital, too. Sashy and I sleep wiff our beds pushed together. Dr JD said we could.'

Summer stood and looked at Jason. 'Separation anxiety?'

He blinked once and then nodded, a little surprised at the question. 'Yes. It's assisted Sasha's recovery no end, having Sally with her all the time.'

Summer nodded. 'She must have undergone a severe trauma to be in a hip spica.'

Jason gave her a quizzical look. 'Are you a medic?'

'I am. I assume you're from Ballarat hospital?'

'You assume correctly.'

Summer nodded. 'Paediatrics?'

'Yes.'

'Short-staffed? Hired any new paediatricians from Sydney lately?'

Jason's brown eyes widened as he continued to look at her. 'Well, *I* haven't personally, but the hospital has. I take it you're our new paediatrician due to start on Monday?'

'You take correctly, Dr Daniels.'

'Brilliant.' He stuck out his hand again and shook hers even more heartily than before. 'Welcome, welcome, welcome.' This time, he put his other hand around hers, enveloping her hand so enthusiastically Summer was overcome by his genuine warmth. Here was a man who had a terrific smile. He was probably another charming smooth talker and she knew just how dangerous that type of man could be. She should do. She'd been married to one.

However, this accidental meeting at least took

care of one stress factor. She no longer needed to worry about meeting her colleagues on Monday, given that she'd just met three of them now.

'We can't wait until Monday.' He leaned a little closer and said quietly, 'Don't want to start tomorrow instead?' Before she could answer, he'd straightened and called to his colleagues. 'Hey, Rhonda, Alyssa.' He turned to tell the nurses about this new discovery and where Summer had expected him to let go of her hands, she was surprised when he didn't.

The feel of her hand within his was starting to make her feel highly self-conscious, especially given that Jason's simple touch was, for some reason, making her heartbeat increase. It was ridiculous. It had to be the mild heat of the day, the crowds, the fact that she'd discovered the man who'd offered to share the bench with her would also be her new colleague. That was the reason her body was behaving in this ridiculous manner. That was all.

Jason was now looking at her again. 'That position has been advertised for the best part of the year and while the year is almost nearing its end, I was thrilled when Admin told me they'd managed to fill the position. We're happy to have you on the team.'

'Thank you.' She glanced down at their hands, then looked pointedly back at him, arching an eyebrow. He was being far too familiar for her liking. Jason followed her eyes and then quickly let go, as though he hadn't realised he was still touching her.

'Sorry.' He shoved his hands into the pockets of his jeans. Why did he feel as though an icy chill had just passed through him? The way she'd looked at him had been a cut-down.

'Thank you. I'm feeling very…welcomed.' Again her words were polite, what you'd expect anyone to say, but there was something reserved, detached about the way she'd said them that made Jason wonder if he was facing another high and mighty princess, such as he'd dealt with in the past.

'Good.' She didn't sound too happy about it but perhaps she was one of those doctors who didn't like to mix the professional and personal, and being here right now definitely mixed them.

'I have to say I'm a little stunned that we should just run into each other in the street like this.'

'You shouldn't be. This is Ballarat, not Sydney. We're a smaller community here. Rhonda, Alyssa and I have known each other since high school. Bradley and Katy here are cousins.' He indicated the children. It was then he realised that Tommy, who was dressed rather formally in a pair of summer trousers with a short-sleeved white shirt, had gone to talk to Bradley. 'Sally and Sasha's parents are the chefs at the hospital's cafeteria, Bradley's mum is a nurse in the surgical department and Bradley's dad and I used to play on the same cricket team when we were eight.'

'Interesting.' She paused and then spoke in a sort of wistful tone, one Jason hadn't expected. 'I don't see anyone I went to high school with and as far as the girls I used to do ballet with, I wouldn't have a clue where they are.' Summer glanced at her son, not surprised he'd gone to talk to Bradley. Tommy had been groomed in the art of making small talk and conversation at an early age. Talking to the boy in the wheel-chair, who looked to be about the same age, was the polite thing to do, and Tommy always did the polite thing.

'You dance?'

'I *danced* when I was a child, yes. I don't do classical any more.'

Jason nodded. There was that icy chill again and he wondered if she was cross with herself for revealing too much. 'Who has any time for anything except working?'

'And taking sick children to watch Christmas lights being turned on.'

'Well…that's working. I have my patients' interests and well-being at heart. An outing like this will lift their spirits and assist with mental and emotional healing which—as we all know—is just as important as physical healing.'

'True. Very true, Dr Daniels.'

'Thank you, Dr Hoyts.'

As she looked away, she was amazed at how such a simple conversation had helped to reassure her that the upheaval would be worth it. Her new colleague appeared quite easygoing and she hoped she'd be able to settle into her new working life with ease. At least that would be one aspect of her life where she wouldn't need to be concerned. Hopefully, here, in this little community, she and Tommy would be able to heal the emotional wounds from their past and move forward into a brighter future because after everything that had taken place, both before and after her husband's death, Summer was desperate to find peace.

'Hey, JD,' Bradley called. 'Guess what?'

'What?' he responded.

'Tommy's going to go to the same school as me! Of course, I won't be there on Monday when he starts because I'll still be in hospital.' Bradley sounded rather despondent at the realisation. 'But we can be friends as soon as I'm back,' he added with enthusiasm.

'Great news,' Jason replied. 'At least Tommy will have one friend at his new school.' He half expected Tommy to be more excited at this but instead the boy maintained a polite smile and nodded rather formally. He seemed a bit... stiff. A bit...hesitant, and Jason thought, 'Like mother, like son.'

'Bradley's had an eye operation,' Tommy remarked to his mother.

'So I can see.' Summer sidestepped Jason so she could give Bradley her attention. Jason watched as she interacted easily with the young boy, knowing what sort of questions to ask him. Well, why wouldn't she? She had a son the same age. Of course she knew what seven-year-old boys were interested in.

She was certainly a beautiful woman. It was the first thing he'd noticed about her when she'd been scanning the crowd for somewhere to sit. She was dressed in a pair of black trousers and a long-sleeved designer shirt which fitted her slim shape. The top few buttons were undone to reveal her slim neckline with the slightest hint of décolletage. She wore a gold cross around her neck and small diamond earrings which sparkled brightly in the artificially lit shopping mall. There was nothing at all overpowering about her ensemble but it screamed class, breeding and elegance.

The whole outfit, from her flat leather shoes to the way she wore her blond hair pulled back into an easy yet effective style with a rhinestone clip, reminded him of Amanda. And he didn't want anyone or anything to remind him of his ex.

It was true that while he could quite easily picture Summer and Amanda chatting about the latest fashions together over a tall decaf cappuccino, he knew he shouldn't tar her with the same brush. However, given her cool and overly polite attitude, he would be wise to be wary. At least she appeared to be able to converse easily with the children and at the moment that was all he really needed to care about. A doctor who could relate to the patients and take some of the workload from his shoulders.

He recalled the memo he'd briefly scanned from the hospital's administration department announcing Summer's appointment. Her résumé had been attached and had stated her marital status as widow. Was Ballarat supposed to be a new beginning for her and her son? Was she still grieving?

He shook his head and forced himself to turn his attention away from the woman before him. Katy wanted to be picked up and he naturally pulled the toddler into his arms and gave her a little cuddle, being careful of the bandage around her head.

He loved kids. Had wanted a gaggle of them but… That was all in his past and he wasn't going to waste the energy opening an old wound. Not tonight. Not when he'd arranged for the children to come and watch the Christmas-tree lights being turned on. They'd had few bright moments in their little lives lately and this outing was something he'd come up with to try to rectify *that* situation at least.

Summer finished her conversation with Bradley and glanced surreptitiously at Jason. He was holding little Katy in the crook of his arm, his strong biceps flexing beneath his light blue polo shirt. He certainly had a good physique—not that she cared about that sort of thing at all. She'd learned the hard way not to fall in love with a man who could grace the pages of the glossy fashion magazines. Men with natural charm, charisma. Men who could talk a woman into believing anything, to make her fall at their feet, only discovering much later what snakes they really were. She'd been there, done that and had the battle scars to prove it. She didn't need it again.

At that moment he looked at her and their eyes held. The people around them seemed to fade into the distance as did the noises, the warmer weather, the flies. It was as though they were inside their own bubble of time and space.

Nothing could touch them. Nothing could separate them. It was the oddest sensation and one Summer had never felt before in her life. It made her tremble deep within, not from fear but from annoyance. How could she possibly be drawn to a man she didn't even know? Ludicrous.

A high-pitched squeal coming from the PA system had both Jason and Summer looking away at the same time. Katy covered her sensitive ears and leaned into Jason as she started to cry. Thankfully, the sound technician sorted it quickly and people started clapping as a local celebrity came to stand, microphone in hand, next to the Christmas tree.

'Here. Let me take her,' Rhonda said to Jason, and took Katy from him. 'I have a nice drink of water here for her and that should help settle the immediate pressure in her ears.'

Jason brushed his hand over Katy's dark brown curls and smiled at her as she started to quieten down. Summer watched, interested to note her new colleague was obviously a man who liked children. That at least was one point in his favour. She'd thought most paediatricians would have such a quality but she'd come across plenty in her time who had no desire to communicate with their little patients but were simply intent on fixing them up and moving them on. Numbers, not names.

'All right, folks,' the announcer said. 'It's almost time to turn on the lights of our Christmas tree. This will, of course, mark the beginning of the Twelve Weeks of Christmas, Ballarat's famous yearly festival in the lead-up to the big day in...' He chuckled. 'You guessed it, twelve weeks' time. Everywhere I've been tonight, everyone I've spoken to has greeted me with a smile on their face and Christmas cheer in their hearts—and we still have twelve more weeks to go! It's great to see.'

'Excuse me, Mum. I can't see properly,' Tommy said. She was about to suggest he stand on the bench next to her when Jason reached out and lifted Tommy off his feet. The boy gasped at the action, his eyes a little wild as he looked at his mother for reassurance.

'Here you go, champ. Up on my shoulders will give you the best view in the place.'

'It's fine, Tommy,' she encouraged. 'You'll be able to see everything from up there.' She took his hand and gave it a little squeeze. Slowly,

Tommy looked around, still wary, but within another moment Summer saw a light come into his eyes as he realised the truth of her words.

'Wow,' he breathed.

The local celebrity with the microphone was announcing the arrival of Miss Ballarat, the winner of the local beauty pageant for that year, and she was driven to the edge of the stage in the back of a white utility truck. When she'd taken her place beside the announcer, he turned to the clapping crowds.

'Are we ready?' the celebrity continued.

The crowd started counting down from twelve—given that this *was* the start of the twelve weeks of Christmas—the atmosphere becoming electric with anticipation as they neared the end. Katy had stopped fussing and was happily sitting on Rhonda's lap, drinking from her special drinking cup. Alyssa was crouched down between Sally and Sasha, the twin girls holding each other's hands with mounting anticipation as they counted backwards. Bradley was clapping in time and Tommy…her son was completely captivated by everything he saw.

She could see quite clearly that he was happy

and she wanted to know how she could get him to be like that on a permanent basis. Ever since his father's death, Tommy had become even more closed off than he'd been before, even more reserved, and she could completely understand why. He hadn't even spoken of his father since that fateful day. Summer had tried so many different things to try to help him, had consulted with child psychologists, had done everything she could think of—including moving to a new town—and *now* he was smiling. Not only smiling but laughing.

'Three. Two. One.'

The switch was flicked. The lights sizzled to life, illuminating one very large Christmas tree. There was a collective gasp of awe and delight from the crowd before everyone broke into a spontaneous round of applause.

It was magical. It was encompassing and for a moment it was as though everyone—just for a second—forgot all their worries and problems as they applauded the beauty and splendour of the sight before them. Summer was no different and smiled up at her son, so happy that he was enjoying himself.

Then her eyes met Jason's. The longer he stared at her, though, the more she began to feel a little uncomfortable. He seemed to be searching for something and what it was, she had no idea. Was he trying to sum her up? To figure out what sort of person she was? What sort of doctor she was? What sort of mother she was? Finally, he spoke. 'Makes you feel as though everything is right with the world. Just for a moment,' he murmured.

Summer nodded, a little surprised by his words. 'That's exactly what I was thinking.'

He didn't look away. 'Wouldn't it be nice if that feeling could continue?'

'It does—for the very young and the very old.'

'While those of us in the middle have to struggle through from one battle to the next.'

'A telling statement,' she remarked.

'And one you appear to understand.'

Her nod was small and she was a little astonished at the turn the conversation had taken.

'Is that why you've come here, Summer? Is that why you've moved to Ballarat?'

'To fight another battle?' she asked rhetorically.

'No. To try to capture the sense of awe and

wonderment. To find a way to harness it, to make it last.'

Summer found herself sighing. 'If only I could. It would indeed be nice but in all honesty, Dr Daniels, I'm just looking for a little bit of peace.'

'A telling statement,' he remarked, using her earlier words, and he was rewarded with a smile, although it wasn't one that met her eyes. He knew she was a widow so life couldn't have been easy for her since her husband's death. Add to that fact that she was now raising her son on her own and he knew—without knowing anything else about her—that she would be facing quite a few more battles in her future. 'I hope you find your peace,' he said softly as he lifted Tommy from his shoulders. Summer was surprised at the tenderness she heard in his voice but instantly dismissed it. Charisma. She didn't need it.

'There you go, champ. Enjoy the show?' Jason asked Tommy.

'Yes. Thank you very much. It was... awesome.' Tommy then turned and started talking more animatedly than before to Bradley, the two of them recounting everything that had just transpired.

'Tommy seems to be a good kid,' Jason remarked. 'Very…polite.'

'He is. My saving grace. I'd be lost without him.' She looked at her son as she spoke.

'Yet you're worried about him.'

She looked back up at Jason. 'What mother isn't worried about their child?'

He nodded and appeared about to say more when they were interrupted by Alyssa who was anxious to get the children back to the hospital before the traffic on the roads started to bank up.

'But this is Ballarat, not Sydney,' Summer pointed out with a small smile. 'Surely peak-hour traffic here would last all of…oh, I don't know…about five to ten minutes?'

'No. It'll be at least fifteen with these crowds,' Jason remarked, deadpan.

He let the light, uplifting sound of her laughter wash over him like a summer breeze. Who was this woman? This woman who he'd be working with? She was beautiful, intelligent and caring. Add to all of that that her sense of humour seemed to be on the same wavelength as his own and Jason realised he could find himself in real danger yet again if he wasn't careful.

Thankfully, though, he knew that looks could be deceiving. That beauty could only be skin deep and that intelligence could be used for bad as well as good purposes.

Still, towards Summer Hoyts he would maintain a polite and professional distance because that way he'd at least be able to ensure his own sanity.

CHAPTER TWO

RHONDA pushed Sasha's wheelchair, Alyssa had Katy in her arms and Sally by her side. Jason pushed Bradley's wheelchair and somehow Summer seemed to fall into step beside them, Tommy's hand firmly in her own as they walked through the crowds back towards the main street where most of the cars were parked.

Tommy was still chatting to Bradley, a little more relaxed than before, and Summer was pleased to see he'd found a new friend. She heard him promising to bring some of his new model cars to the hospital as soon as they'd been unpacked.

'What's Sydney like?' Bradley asked, excitement in his face. 'I'll bet it's totally buzzin'' and, hey—have you been to the Opera House? Or the Sydney Harbour Bridge? Have you seen the bridge?'

Tommy merely shrugged. 'We could see both the bridge and the Opera House from our penthouse where we lived.' There wasn't much enthusiasm in her son's tone because to him the classic Australian icons weren't all that special. Not when you saw them day in, day out.

'Penthouse?'

'It's just where we lived.'

'Yeah, but have you *driven* across the bridge? I think that'd be totally buzzin'. I want to go to Sydney one day when I'm bigger and I'm gonna drive my own car over the bridge.' Bradley's delight wasn't to be brushed aside.

'My driver used to drive me over the bridge every day to get to school.'

'You had a *driver*?' Bradley was now in awe. Jason was listening interestedly as well. So Summer had lived in an inner-city penthouse, one which had afforded a good view of the harbour. He knew how expensive those places were and what sort of income you needed to live there. Did she come from money? Had she married money? She certainly had the quality about her, the one that said she was used to giving orders and having them followed. And if she'd been living a life of luxury, what on earth was she doing here in Ballarat? The more he thought about her, the more questions he seemed to have.

'Yeah. It was no big deal,' Tommy continued. 'We had a maid and a cook and a butler as well but we don't have them now. It's just me and Mum.'

Summer was busy trying to decipher her son's tone, to give her some sort of clue as to his feelings. He was obedient, careful and intelligent but he also played his cards close to his chest. She'd tried to talk to him, to get him to open up, but apart from talking to her about his love of cars and showing her the things he built out of his building bricks, Tommy didn't ever venture his opinion or thoughts.

She knew it no doubt stemmed from her husband's attitude that 'children should be seen and not heard'. There was also the fact that as heir to the Hoyts fortune, he'd been told from a very early age that his destiny was to run the family business, to take his rightful place in society, that nothing mattered more than money and status.

Tommy had also been given everything he'd ever needed or ever wanted as far as material possessions went, but he hadn't been given love and approval from his father and she was positive that was one of the main things he'd always craved.

Summer was so busy concentrating on Tommy that she completely missed the way Jason's eyebrows had arched at Tommy's disclosure. So Summer had definitely lived the designer, closed-set lifestyle in Sydney. He'd picked it up from her clothes and the way she carried herself but he hadn't realised she'd come from *that* much money. Why Ballarat? What had made her come here? The question didn't seem to go away, no matter how hard he tried to shake it.

Perhaps she had friends here? Family? Or had she simply done something completely spontaneous and stuck a pin in the map of Australia and moved to wherever it had landed? No. Her kind were rarely spontaneous. Then again, the answer could be as simple as she'd needed to make a fresh start after her husband's death. Somewhere new. Somewhere different.

He shook his head, doubting she'd stay. After the glitz and glamour of Sydney, she'd find Ballarat dull and boring in comparison. Besides, it was none of his business and he'd do well to stop trying to speculate what had prompted her to come here. The point was that she *had* come to Ballarat, she *had* been offered and *had* accepted the position of resident paediatrician, which was just what the department, and more importantly, himself, required. Starting Monday, his own workload would be halved and between the two of them and their two training registrars, they'd be able to get on top of things that had been moving far too slowly in the past.

That was all he needed to be worried about. She was here. She was willing to do the job. Her past didn't concern him…and neither did her future.

They'd arrived at the two hospital vans, which were equipped to take wheelchairs, and Alyssa turned to face Summer.

'If you're not busy, why don't you come back to the hospital with us to have a look at the ward, meet a few of the other patients?'

'Uh…' Summer glanced at Jason but he was busy helping Bradley out of the wheelchair and into the van. 'I don't know if that's possible at the moment.'

Tommy looked up at her with wide eyes. 'Please, Mum? Bradley and I can talk for a bit longer and it would be good manners to accept.'

Summer looked down at her son. He rarely asked for anything and the fact that he was asking to spend more time to converse further with Bradley tugged at her heartstrings. He had made a friend. *That* was a breakthrough in itself. She found herself accepting Alyssa's invitation.

'At least it will stop me from getting lost on Monday.'

'Can I go in the van with Bradley?' Tommy asked again.

'If that's OK with Dr Daniels.'

'Sure,' Jason replied.

'That would be…totally buzzing,' was Tommy's reply, and Summer smiled in surprise to hear those words coming out of his mouth. 'Thank you, Dr Daniels.'

'No problem, champ, and you can call me JD

or Dr JD if you like. That's what the other kids do. Climb aboard.'

Tommy looked to Bradley and both of them said, 'Totally buzzin',' in unison before laughing as though it was the funniest thing in the world. Tommy climbed into the back of the van and buckled himself into the seat next to Bradley.

'Where did you park?' Jason asked her.

'I didn't. Tommy and I caught the bus. It goes from right outside our apartment into the centre of the city, dropping us off right near the mall.'

He was surprised at that. He'd half expected her to hire a limousine from Melbourne. He was intrigued to find she appeared quite practical. Although perhaps her chosen mode of transport was more of a novelty, given that she was used to having a driver to take her everywhere. 'Sounds as though you did your homework.'

'I'm not one for surprises, especially where public transport is concerned.'

'You don't drive?'

'Oh, I do. I just couldn't be bothered with the hassle of driving in a strange town and parking in unfamiliar car parks. Plus, I knew I'd avoid this.' She indicated the people around them, all getting into their cars and having to wait to exit their spots.

'Fair enough. Well...' He opened the passenger door for her. 'If you'll permit me, ma'am, I'd be more than honoured to be your driver for the evening. After all, being from the hospital, we get priority parking and I know these streets very well.' He held out his hand and Summer found herself hesitating for a moment, knowing if she touched him again, her body would no doubt be smitten with tingles as it had been before. However much she wanted to reject touching him, she knew it would be impolite and she was never impolite. She took his hand, accepting his help, and wasn't disappointed in the tingles. 'Thank you, Dr Daniels.'

'Jason. We're quite informal here.'

She watched him walk around to the driver's door and then check that everyone was buckled in before heading off. She still preferred to call him Dr Daniels because at least that way she felt as though she had more distance between them yet she also knew it would make her stand out more if she didn't do as he asked and call him by his first name.

'So where's your apartment?'

'Two blocks from the hospital. The administrator was very helpful in assisting us to find something nice and close. There's a school bus which goes from the end of our street to Tommy's school so that's a bonus.'

'Two blocks from the hospital?'

'Davies Street. Do you know it?' She held up her hand before he could answer. 'Sorry. Of course. You've already told me you know the streets of Ballarat like the back of your hand.'

'And I know Davies Street as intimately as the hairs on the back of my hand.' He held up his big, manly hand as if to prove it before looking over at Summer with a smile. 'I live in Davies Street, too.'

'Really?' Ballarat really was quite small. 'What number?'

'Sixty-four. Apartment two.'

'You are joking?' Her tone was dead serious. 'We live in apartment three. We're across the hall from you.'

He nodded slowly. 'Sounds that way. I should

have guessed. I was the one who told Admin there was an apartment vacant and I do recall seeing a moving van pull up yesterday morning as I rushed off to the hospital.'

'So we're neighbours.' Summer sighed, not at all sure how she felt about that. Ever since she'd met Jason Daniels, she'd felt an instant pull of attraction towards him, like nothing she'd ever felt before. She'd told herself that it meant nothing, that she would be professional, work with him during their shifts and then go home to her apartment and her son. Now, though, even when she was at home, Jason would only be across the hall. So close. They'd bump into each other in the hallways, or when they collected their mail. He could come over at any time and ask her for a cup of sugar—if he needed sugar, that was.

'You don't sound too thrilled about it.' Jason hadn't been too happy either. How was he supposed to keep his distance when she would be everywhere he turned? Even now, sitting next to her, her fresh scent, which was a mixture of wildflowers and promise, was settling around him. It was alluring, as was the expanse of neck she was displaying. He wondered what she'd look like with her lovely blond tresses floating around her shoulders, framing her face.

He stopped at a red light just outside the hospital entrance and forced his thoughts to stop as well. Imagining how Summer Hoyts looked with her hair down, being affected by her perfume, by her nearness wasn't going to happen. He'd had enough heartache to last him for quite some time and he didn't need another helping.

'I'm sorry. I didn't mean to sound so...unenthusiastic. At least Tommy and I will know someone in our building. That's a good thing when you've just moved to a new town.'

The light turned green and Jason pulled into the hospital's driveway. 'Do you know anyone else here?'

'No. Not a soul.'

He turned off the engine before shifting in his seat to face her for a moment. 'Then, if you don't mind me asking, why Ballarat?'

Summer shrugged. 'The hospital needed a paediatrician. I'm qualified for the position and...' She paused for a moment, not sure she should say anything else but decided it didn't really matter. 'And I needed to get out of Sydney.'

'You needed a change?'

'A big change. So did Tommy.' At the mention of her son, Jason turned to look at the two boys, who were still chatting quite animatedly about the latest Porsche 911. Tommy had the same colouring as his mother—blond hair, blue eyes. But where Tommy's were a light blue, Summer's were darker, more intense and when he looked at her again, he saw a hint of the pain she'd no doubt been through.

Unable to stop himself, he reached out and touched Summer's shoulder. 'I'm sorry for your loss. I know, from your hospital file, that you're a widow.'

She gasped and for a second he wasn't sure whether it was due to his words or his touch. He hadn't missed the fact that every time they'd come into contact there had been an increasing awareness between them. He quickly removed his hand, having only meant to touch her in a compassionate way.

'Yes. Cameron, my husband, died eighteen months ago.'

'That can't have been at all easy for you.'

'Or for Tommy.' She looked at her son. 'This is the brightest I've seen him in such a long time.'

Jason's smile was natural as he watched the boys in his rear-view mirror. 'That must help reassure you that your move here was the right thing to do.'

'It does and you have no idea how many times I've questioned myself since we left Sydney the other day. I know we both still have a long way to go with the healing process but this is definitely a positive beginning.'

And that was another reason why Jason should keep his distance. Not only for his own sake but for Summer's as well. She was a grieving widow and no doubt wasn't looking for anything else relationship-wise. He was a bitter divorcé who didn't need to be thinking about his attractive but aloof new neighbour.

Professional colleagues. Perhaps, given a little more time, they could become friends but it was obvious neither of them needed anything else. Besides, he doubted whether she'd be here for that long. She'd soon realise that the big-city lights, the parties, the fashion parades would be missing from the new life she attested to wanting. No. There would be no point in getting to know her better. No point at all.

By the end of her first week at work, Summer knew without a doubt that she'd made the right decision to leave Sydney. It was a comforting fact to know she was not only capable of making such decisions on her own but that they also turned out to be correct. The knowledge certainly went a long way to boosting her flagging self-confidence.

As far as medicine and treating her patients went, she always knew where she stood, but in her own personal life things hadn't always gone as planned. When she'd told her friends that she was leaving Sydney, they'd all told her she was mad, that she was still too lost in the five steps of grieving to know her own mind. They'd told her she was a bad mother to be ripping her child away from everything he'd ever known to take him to some small town where he probably wouldn't have access to high-speed Internet services.

And that was just her friends! When she'd informed Cameron's parents of her decision, they'd been furious. How dare she take their only grandchild away, especially given the fact that he was a *Hoyts* and as such he not only had responsibilities to the community at large but also to the future of the Hoyts company?

As it turned out, Tommy had spent less time on the computer during the past week than ever before. Instead, he preferred to come to the children's ward with her after school and play cars with Bradley and the other children on the ward. He was interacting more with children his age, talking more about his cars and eating and sleeping better than he had for the past year and a half.

Bradley was due to go home tomorrow, his eye having healed well from the extensive laser surgery he'd undergone over a week ago.

'He's taken a little longer to recover than I anticipated, but his vision is good and altogether he's been very lucky that there wasn't any permanent damage to the eye,' Jason remarked.

Summer had read up on Bradley's notes to discover the seven-year-old had been in an accident at school where a sharp object had pierced the eye. He'd been flown to

Melbourne's Children's Hospital where, once the surgery had been performed, they'd sent him back to Ballarat for follow-up.

'I think your Tommy has certainly helped with boosting Bradley's spirits. Coming in before and after school to play with him. It's been really good for Bradley,' Jason continued as he stood near her at the nurses' station in the paediatric ward. Summer was watching the two boys in the playroom.

'And likewise Bradley's done Tommy the world of good. He's found a real friend. I just hope it continues once Bradley leaves here and returns to school.'

'I'm sure it will but you know how it is when you're young. You can change your best friend almost every week and still be happy within yourself.'

Summer shook her head as she continued to watch her son, her words spoken in an almost absent-minded way. 'Not my Tommy. He doesn't make friends easily.'

'Really? I find that hard to believe. He seems quite a personable boy.'

Summer turned to look at Jason, nodding her

gratitude at the compliment. 'He's polite. He knows how to make small talk and that sort of thing. Enough to get him by, but making real, long-lasting friends…' She looked at Tommy again and slowly shook her head. Jason watched her closely, wondering if she wasn't also talking about herself.

Summer had maintained her poise and calm during this first week and while she appeared quite relaxed with not only the staff in the paediatric ward but their patients as well, she'd been rather short, sometimes even blunt with him. Never rude but direct and to the point. It was as though with him she was all business. Nothing more.

He knew it was wise not to be concerned about it. After all, he wanted to keep his distance from his intriguing colleague but her son also fascinated him. There was something about the boy that wasn't quite right and to hear Summer say that he found it difficult to make friends only confirmed his thoughts.

'He didn't have close friends in Sydney?'

'He had friends…school friends…although I guess you could say they were more like acquaintances, but I've never seen him bond with anyone the way he has with Bradley.'

'Why do you think that is?'

'Why he's so distant?' Summer thought for a moment, a frown peppering her brow. 'Possibly because his father was so distant. I've often wondered whether Tommy thought that was the way he was supposed to behave. Taking his cues from his father.' She sighed. 'Trying to act the same as his father in the hope of winning his approval, his attention.'

Jason was surprised to hear her talk that way. It was the first inkling he'd received that perhaps not everything had been all sunshine and roses with her marriage. Or perhaps it was simply that Tommy and his father hadn't bonded.

Summer snapped out of it and shook her head. 'Sorry. I didn't mean to think out loud like that.' Her smile was an embarrassed one but Jason waved her concerns away, trying not to focus on how incredible she looked when her smile was a natural one.

'Don't worry about it.' It had been a moment, to show him that perhaps there was more to Summer Hoyts than he'd initially thought, and that wasn't what he wanted. He was a man who needed distance from women like Summer. She wasn't exactly the same as his ex-wife but he'd been fooled once and he wasn't going to be fooled again. Even if he did dig a little deeper beneath Summer's surface and find something other than pure ice, it wouldn't matter. He wasn't getting back into the ring. He wasn't risking his heart. Not again. Not for anyone. He and love didn't mix and he'd learned that lesson the hard way.

'Anyway, as you say, it's good to see Tommy making such good friends with Bradley.' He shifted some papers on the desk. 'I'm sure when they're back at school on Monday, they'll be as thick as thieves.' Jason looked at the clock. 'We have about half an hour before Friday morning ward round begins. What time does Tommy's school bus come?'

'Oh, help. Is that the time?' Summer burst into action and headed off to get her son. Jason watched the way she moved. It was with the same grace and poise he'd observed during the week, even though now she was rushing and a little agitated. It was good to see her feathers ruffled a little.

By the time the ward round began, she was back, her working clothes, which consisted of a pair of three-quarter-length trousers and a knit top, looking uncreased and immaculate. She'd worn her hair up for work every day and Jason was now more than a little interested to see what she looked like with it down.

At their apartment complex, they hadn't even run into each other once. Of course, Summer had no doubt spent most of her non-working hours unpacking and getting things set up and out of the boxes, but he had to confess he'd been a little disappointed not to have even bumped into her now and then. He'd caught himself on several occasions wondering what it might be like to see her dressed more comfortably, more casually than the designer labels she seemed to prefer.

What did she look like when she was cooking dinner? Sitting and relaxing? Reading a book? Did she ever relax back in her favourite chair and put her feet up on the coffee-table? What sort of food did she like? Was she a good cook or did she prefer to order in? There were so many questions he had about her and while he didn't want to have them at all, he'd come to the acceptance somewhere around three o'clock that morning that he was indeed quite fascinated by his new colleague. He didn't want to be, but he was.

One question he often found himself pondering was what would she look like first thing in the morning, all tousled from sleep. And that sort of thought was of the dangerous variety because it bordered between a healthy curiosity and the line he'd drawn which shouldn't be crossed at any point.

He'd first met Amanda at a hospital function where she'd held the position of Miss Ballarat, brought in to cut the ribbon as they'd opened a new department. Jason recalled he'd been equally as intrigued by her as well, asking himself many of the same questions he was now asking of Summer. Now, though, he had all the answers where Amanda was concerned, and look how that first foray into the world of love had turned out.

He forced himself to look away from Summer as she chatted with little Sally. The paediatric ward rounds were often longer and far less formal than on other wards because it was healthy for the children to want to interact with their doctors. Indeed, as head of department, Jason seemed to encourage it and Summer was pleased about that. The children's mental well-being was vitally important and it appeared that she'd found another paediatrician who was on her wavelength.

She said as much as the ward round finished and they headed off to the public day clinic, which was in the next building. 'It's a very friendly department.'

'Do I detect a note of surprise, Dr Hoyts?'

'It's a good surprise.'

'Your hospital in Sydney was more formally run?'

'You could say that. Everything by the book for every department as decreed by Administration, *unless* you have a department head who's willing to buck the system and, of course, no one is willing to do that because they're all too afraid they're going to lose their jobs.'

'Let me guess, your head of department didn't want to lose his job.'

'No. Add to that fact that he kept thinking I was there to spy on him, to report him if he stepped out of line, and some days it wasn't the nicest atmosphere to work in.'

'Why? Why on earth would he think you'd do that?' Jason held open the door to the clinic for her. Summer looked around briefly but her thoughts were centred on Jason's question.

'Because before my husband's death, he was the hospital's administrator.' Summer said the words with a frown, then picked up her first set of case notes and called her patient through to the waiting room.

She saw two children who had otitis media, three who she diagnosed with asthma and another few who presented with suspicious rashes. There was also a child with a suspected fractured thumb whose mother hadn't deemed it necessary to take him to the A and E department. Summer sent them to Radiology with X-ray request forms and then quickly scanned the patient's notes in case it gave her any clues as to the boy's previous medical history.

The last few entries had been written in Jason's neat and legible handwriting which stated he wanted the boy—Ashley—to be closely monitored and any further bone breaks or incidents to be reported both to himself and Social Services.

Summer picked up the notes and headed down the corridor to Jason's consulting room. She knocked twice and when he called for her to come in, she was pleased to find him alone.

'Hi. How's it going?' he asked as he stood and stretched his arms up and over his head, closing his eyes for a moment. Summer watched as the white cotton shirt pulled tight across his long, firm body and she couldn't help but admire his physique. He didn't wear a tie and the collar of his shirt was unbuttoned and open, the bottom of his shirt was starting to come untucked, his trousers riding a little lower on his hips.

She swallowed, astonished to find she couldn't look away. The man had been on her mind more often than not this past week and that was something she hadn't expected. She found herself listening near her front door for sounds coming from across the hall but given the apartment had been built with strong, sturdy walls, she hadn't been able to hear anything. It was ridiculous. It was silly and schoolgirlish but even now, watching him stretch like this, Summer was starting to realise that she really was attracted to Jason, rather than simply being intrigued by him, as she'd initially thought.

'So. What can I do for you?'

She closed her eyes, wondering if he'd seen her staring at his body before deciding she'd better ignore the entire thing, wipe the vision from her mind and get on with her job.

'Are you all right, Summer?'

Her eyes snapped open. 'Yes. Fine.' She held out Ashley's case notes to him. 'You've written that you wanted to be notified.'

'Ah. Ashley Jones. Right. Thanks.' He quickly scanned what she'd written. 'Did his mother actually take him to Radiology?'

'I sent her down there.'

Jason quickly picked up the phone and dialled the other department, relaxing a little when it was confirmed that the patient was indeed there. 'Send an orderly back to the clinic with them to ensure they return for further consultation,' Jason instructed, before replacing the receiver and dialling Social Services. When that was done, he looked at Summer. 'Do you mind if I sit in on the rest of the consultation?'

'Not at all. If you'd prefer to take the case over, I don't have a problem with that at all.'

'No. Chances are Mrs Jones asked specifically to see you because you're the new doctor and wouldn't know what was going on.'

Summer nodded. 'I've seen this sort of ploy before. How many other doctors has she taken Ashley to in the hope of covering her tracks?'

'I don't think it's her tracks she's covering. The family only moved to town six months ago and Ashley's older brother has been arrested twice for unruly public behaviour.'

'Older brother? Single-parent family?'

'No. Frank, who works in A and E, told me that Mr Jones has been in for several minor injuries, all of which were explained away as mere clumsiness.'

'Whoa. Are you saying that the older son rules the roost?'

'Literally. Ashley coming in might, unfortunately, be the leverage we need to finally get Social Services involved. Being a minor, we have cause to investigate. Thanks for letting me know.'

'It's all right. Just doing my job.'

'And doing it well, from all accounts. I haven't heard a bad word against you all week long.' There was a teasing smile playing across his lips and it only enhanced his good looks.

Summer raised an eyebrow, ignoring the way her stomach seemed to churn with excited butterflies. 'Expecting bad reports?'

'Well, you know you big-city types. Chances are you could have waltzed in here and started insisting we change the way we do things because usually the big-city way is the only way to go.'

'You've had other doctors doing that?'

'We've had a lot of locums from Melbourne who think it's their job to come here and educate us small-town hicks in the latest paediatric techniques, most of which don't work in such a relaxed environment as we employ here at Ballarat Hospital.'

'At least you have happy patients here. Sasha, for example, is continuing to make an excellent recovery, given that Sally's allowed to be with her at all times. Even this morning they were arguing about one of the dolls, trying to decide which colour dress she looked best in. Honestly, Jason, even something as small and as natural as arguing with your sister can help the healing process.'

'You sound as though you know what you're talking about. Do you have siblings?'

'Er…no.' She'd been caught off guard by the personal question. 'I'm an only child. I was merely speaking from my medical observations. Newborn babies need to be touched. Toddlers and young children need interaction and plenty of attention.'

'And siblings need to squabble. You're right. I'm not trying to contradict or criticise you. I have a sister. She's two years younger than me and I have to say that growing up we were the best of friends and the best of enemies.'

'And as adults?'

Jason's smile was completely natural as he spoke of his sister. 'Definitely the best of friends and because I grew up with a sibling, it means I have an understanding of how to fight fair, how to say I'm sorry and how to forgive.'

There was something about his words, a gut-wrenching honesty which touched Summer deeply. 'You make me quite envious. Not only for myself but for Tommy.'

'You want more children?'

Summer shrugged sadly but forced a smile. 'I did. It didn't happen. That's all in the past now. I have Tommy and I love him very much.'

'It's very evident.' Jason knew he was starting to edge over that line he'd drawn but couldn't help himself. 'My wife didn't want children.'

'You're married?' Summer was instantly shocked by his words. She hadn't even thought to ask, to check. She quickly schooled her features, immediately apologising. 'I'm sorry, Jason. It's none of my bu—'

'I'm divorced,' he interjected quickly.

'Oh.'

'Yeah. Oh.'

'Nasty divorce?' she couldn't help but ask. He'd started the conversation, so she presumed it was all right for her to find out just a little bit more. Purely for business purposes, she reasoned with herself. She wouldn't want to make a horrible *faux pas* at any time.

'Yes.'

They stood there, looking at each other, the desk between them. It was a look of open honesty and Summer was astonished to realise that Jason had wanted her to know his marital status. Had wanted her to know that he was single.

His rich brown eyes were filled with a mixture of relief and curiosity along with a definite appreciation for the person standing before him. The insane thing was that Summer was absolutely positive her eyes were portraying the exact same information to him.

It was ridiculous. It was crazy but it was there.

CHAPTER THREE

THE PHONE on Jason's desk rang, breaking the moment.

He quickly snatched it up while Summer closed her eyes, unable to believe she'd just been caught in yet another such moment with a man she barely knew. She needed to slow things down, to take a huge step back from him, literally as well as figuratively.

During her courtship with Cameron, she'd made fast and hasty decisions, all of which she'd managed to justify under the guise that she'd been in love with him. They'd met at the hospital and he'd made her feel alive for the first time in a very long time. Since her parents' death, she'd been so sad, almost a shell of her former self, but somehow Cameron had brought her back to life again.

They'd laughed at the same things. Enjoyed

the same taste in movies and books. Appreciated the same fine art. It had been a wonderful time in her life. She only wished now she'd been able to see it for the farce that it had been. She hadn't realised her husband was also good at acting the part of the doting suitor when all he'd really been after had been her own family fortune.

'Money should breed with money,' he'd once told her, his words harsh. 'You had a sizeable fortune, my dear. Did you think we'd let anyone come along and marry you?'

When she'd questioned him further, even though his words had been driving one dagger after the next into her love-stricken heart, he'd told her their marriage had been more of a business merger than anything else.

'When your parents died, my father watched their shares and stocks. When the time was right, when you were worth your most, he told me to start romancing you.'

'No!' She'd rejected his words and all he'd done had been to laugh cruelly before he'd left the room. She'd been duped. She'd fallen for his good looks, his smile, his smooth-talking charm, and she'd paid the price.

She'd made a mess out of her past but she wasn't about to make a mess out of her future. She was the type of person who learned from her mistakes and she wasn't going to make another with the man before her.

The attraction, the physical tug she felt towards him was just that—physical attraction. She didn't need to act on it and, in fact, things in her life would no doubt go from bad to worse if she did. Emotional involvement with a colleague wasn't on her 'to do' list right now.

Jason returned the receiver to its cradle and Summer looked up at him, straightening her shoulders, back in professional mode, thoughts of everything except her job banished from her mind.

'That was Radiology. They've done a rush job on the X-rays of Ashley's hand and apparently Mrs Jones was ready to bolt so they're being accompanied back here now. I've told them to bring them straight through to my consulting room. So take a seat and I'll check to see if the social worker can come immediately so we can all see Ashley together.'

Jason picked up the phone again and began making arrangements. It was imperative that they get Ashley Jones sorted out immediately and he was pleased he had something to focus on other than thinking about the moment he'd just shared with Summer.

He'd been a little surprised and secretly pleased when she'd given him a visual caress when he'd been stretching. It was good to know she wasn't as immune to him as he'd thought but to say he'd been astounded to read what was so clearly displayed in her glorious blue eyes was an understatement. Although when he'd looked at her just now after talking to Radiology, her eyes had told a different story. She had herself back under control and he didn't blame her one bit.

His call was connected and he returned his focus to the situation at hand. Focus on work, he had to keep reminding himself, and it was the fact that those reminders were needed every time he was near Summer that was starting to concern him.

Soon the little consulting room was filled with several different people, all impressing the need on Mrs Jones to take action against her oldest son. They could all see how scared she was and it was decided that once Ashley's cast had been applied, they should contact Mr Jones so that the entire family could find sanctuary together.

'Well, that was certainly a different sort of clinic,' Summer said with a relieved sigh as she met Jason walking back to the paediatric ward. Naturally, they'd run a little over time but it was nothing she wasn't used to.

'You can say that again, although I'm extremely pleased with the outcome. Let's hope that the psychologists can also help Ashley's big brother through whatever anger is causing him to be so abusive.'

They'd reached the nurses' station and Summer looked at Jason in approval. 'You really care, don't you? Not just about Ashley but about the whole family.'

'There's no point in just sticking a plaster on the wound if it hasn't been debrided properly.'

She smiled at his analogy. 'I agree with you one hundred per cent, Jason.'

He gave her a puzzled look and scratched his head. 'You know, Summer, that's about the third time you've alluded to approval of my methods, which leads me to wonder what sort of people you were working with in Sydney. I know you said you had a head of unit who didn't want to buck the system in case your husband found out, but what about the other members of staff? Were they equally as rigid?'

'You mean the ones who were more concerned with budgets and projections rather than patient care. Of course there were staff members, few and far between, who felt otherwise but I'm sorry to report that it was definitely a minority but it was that minority that kept me there. Generally, people had the view that if it was too much trouble, hand it over to another department.'

'Which is essentially what I've done here,' he felt compelled to point out.

'No. You didn't just pass on the whole sticky mess, Jason, you facilitated the first step in fixing the lines of communication and I have no doubt that you'll continue to be involved, even if it's behind the scenes in conferring with both the psychology and social-work departments. You're a hands-on doctor and you personally care.'

'And you're the same. I can tell.'

Her smile increased at the compliment, her

eyes brightened, and Jason felt as though he'd taken a hit to the solar plexus. 'Thank you.' Summer looked around the ward and was amazed to feel a sense of belonging. It was as though she'd finally found a place where people thought the same way, behaved the same way, employed the same values as herself. It was not only exciting and stimulating but also quite refreshing.

'So, if you weren't happy at your hospital in Sydney, why did you wait so long to leave? Was it just so you could fight the good fight?' Jason couldn't help but ask the question. It had been playing on his mind since she'd made those comments earlier.

Summer shrugged, strangely not annoyed that he was prying into her personal life. It was as though he was really interested in her, in *wanting* to get to know her, and that in itself was a nice feeling to have—the feeling that someone was actually interested in you. No one had seriously been interested in her for far too long.

'That, and I guess it was force of habit. It was also easier. Cameron accepted the fact that I worked there as it was a prestigious hospital. If I'd tried to go anywhere else…' She trailed off and shook her head. 'It wasn't worth the headache.'

'And did you stay on at the same hospital after your husband's death?'

'I did. It seemed…I don't know, the right thing to do at the time.' Summer frowned and thought for a second. 'I didn't really know what to do, actually, so I just kept on living my life. Day after day. Night after night. All of it without Cameron. All of it with a strange sort of numbness around my life. And then there was Tommy. Naturally, I was concerned about him, about effecting more change in his life at that point. He was only five and a half and while a lot goes over their heads at that age, after Cameron's death he clammed up completely. He never talked about his dad, still doesn't. It was as though now that Cameron wasn't in our lives, he wasn't worth remembering.'

'That must have hurt you.'

'It made me sad. Sad for Tommy. Every little boy should have a dad who thinks he's special.'

'True. In fact, every child should be told just how special and unique they are.'

'Quite. I do my best. I really do.' Summer sat

down and began fiddling with a pen. Jason had asked her a personal question and they appeared to be having quite an open and frank discussion so she decided that gave her permission to ask him about his own life. 'Did your parents make you feel special?'

Jason's smile was automatic. 'They did. Not only me but my sister as well. In fact, that's their job.'

'What? Making you and your sister feel special?'

He chuckled. 'No. They run a childminding centre here at the hospital.'

'Rent-A-Grand? Tommy's enrolled to go there sometimes when I'm working.'

'Then you can rest assured that he'll be well taken care of.'

'By your parents, who make every child feel special.' She nodded her approval again. 'I really did make the right decision in coming here.'

'You doubted yourself?'

'It was the first major decision I've ever made and…well, let's just say I received quite a lot of…flak over it.'

'From your family?'

'I don't have any family.' She brushed his words away. 'No. Mainly from Cameron's parents. Also from my friends. They all thought I was suffering from delusions, that I was depressed over Cameron's death and that I was lashing out by doing something so completely out of character. I'm sure they expected me to be admitted to the psych ward before the packing had finished.'

'Sounds like you have some really supportive mates.' His words were said with a hint of sarcasm but she also detected a touch of sadness. 'Sorry, Summer,' he instantly apologised. 'I shouldn't have made that crack about your friends.'

'It's fine, Jason. It's exactly what I thought. All I received was opposition, everywhere I turned, and in the end I didn't say goodbye to anyone.'

'Oh, Summer.' He'd heard the note of disappointment in her tone as she'd spoken and now, as he took a step closer, he could see that her eyes had glazed over with tears. He took the pen from her hand and, pulling her to her feet, wrapped her in a warm, supportive hug.

She found her arms going around him of their own volition. His body was warm, firm and comfortable. She knew he wasn't trying to make a pass at her, knew he didn't mean anything by the embrace except to show her he cared. And it was nice. In fact, it was so nice that she felt the tears she'd previously managed to hold back slide down her cheeks. She pushed him away before it turned into a waterfall.

She sniffed and reached for a tissue, turning her face away from him.

'Hey. It's OK. I didn't mean to upset you.'

'I'm not upset.' She forced herself to look at him. 'Honestly, I'm not. Sometimes, though, an act of pure kindness brings with it strong emotions.'

Jason watched as she gave him a watery smile and the message sank in that what Summer needed the most was friendship. Not only from himself but from the people around her, her new colleagues and neighbours. She was a highly vulnerable woman who was obviously in turmoil. The man in him wanted to stay away, to run for the hills because vulnerable women had a way of sucking you in then spitting you out. Yet the doctor in him wanted to help, wanted to heal her. She needed to be built up, to feel strong and secure in her own opinions and decisions. She needed to feel she was both special and unique and for those reasons alone he must quash the attraction he felt for her.

For the next two weeks, Summer was pleased with the way her new life was turning out. She'd been fortunate to have the weekends off, meaning that she and Tommy had been free to attend some of the Christmas activities which were part of the Twelve Weeks of Christmas. When they'd been attending a function held at Lake Wendouree, they'd seen and heard real kookaburras 'laughing' in the big gumtrees. Both she and Tommy had been delighted as if they'd wanted to see a kookaburra in Sydney, they'd have had to go to the zoo.

The shops were starting to become filled with Christmas shoppers and the hospital was organising its own contribution to the famous Ballarat festival. In a few weeks' time, the hospital would be the major sponsor of a charity ball. It was the talk of the department and the women were starting to discuss what they would wear.

Summer listened with interest to the conversations, joining in here and there but mostly enjoying the buzz the event created. 'It's as though it's the last year of high school and you're all excited about what dress you should buy,' she commented to Rhonda.

'Absolutely. This is the one time of the year my husband doesn't complain about me spending money on an expensive outfit.' Alyssa agreed and the two women laughed. Summer's mind automatically thought about Cameron and how, when they'd first started to date, he'd been quite critical of her outfits, telling her that if she was going to be with him, she needed to be immaculately groomed at all times. Of course, he'd sprinkled smiles and encouragement over his words, taking her shopping to show her what he'd meant.

After their engagement had been announced, she'd not only entered the world of the chauffeur-driven car but had been introduced to her future mother-in-law's personal designer. A complete make-over had transpired and Summer, who'd never been concerned with fashion, especially during her university and medical school days, had been taught the ins and outs, the dos and don'ts of the fashion world.

At first it had been fun, exciting and quite interesting. Years later, having to be immaculately groomed at all times, especially as she had become the hospital director's wife, had become much less fun. She'd had shoes, dresses, outfits and jewellery. Everything a woman would ever want, but she hadn't had the love of her husband.

'How about you?' Alyssa asked, bringing Summer out of her reverie.

'Huh?'

'What are you planning to wear to the ball?'

'Uh…I have no idea. In fact, I haven't really given it much thought.'

'Well, you should. I know a certain doctor who would be quite happy to see you all dressed up in your finest clothes.'

'Really?' Summer was astonished. 'Who?'

Rhonda looked at Alyssa with incredulity before both women turned to look at Summer again and said in unison, 'Jason, you ninny.'

'What! No. No, no, no. Jason and I are just colleagues.'

'Ri-i-i-ght.' Alyssa and Rhonda looked at each other and winked.

'We believe you.'

'Thousands wouldn't.'

'Would do him the world of good, too,' Rhonda added. 'The poor man hasn't been on a date in years. Ever since *she* left.'

'Leave him alone,' Alyssa defended. 'His divorce was only final about six months ago and JD is the type of man to love deeply. Emotionally scarred, he is.'

Rhonda nodded then her smile returned. 'And what he needs is to go to the ball with the newest addition to our little family. It would do him good.'

Summer had listened to the two women, interested in what they had to say. Jason seemed a bit of an enigma. He seemed to switch between being friendly and caring to giving her a wide berth.

'His ex-wife was a model,' Rhonda told her. 'A lot like you in some ways. Always pretty and immaculate.'

Summer tried not to cringe at the word.

'She had ambition, that one,' Alyssa agreed with a nod. 'Still does.'

'She's still working as a model?' Summer asked.

'Oh, yes. Quite famous now is the former Miss Ballarat. Which is why it would do him good to get out and about. He needs to stop thinking about things and have more fun, and to do that the simplest answer is for him to ask you to the dance.'

Alyssa sighed. 'You'd make a gorgeous-looking couple. His tall, dark and handsome looks, your startling blond hair and mesmerising blue eyes.'

Both women looked off into the distance and sighed.

Summer shook her head. She wasn't used to this sort of good-natured teasing and decided the best course of action was to laugh it off. 'You two are, quite simply, crazy.' Although their words did stick in her head. Jason? Was Jason really *interested* in her? Or was she the nearest single female and so people would just presume they'd get together? No. The two nurses had to be wrong. In any case, he wasn't her type.

'Thank you. Thank you very much,' Rhonda

replied, as she stood and went to check on a little girl who had started to cry. Just then Jason came up and sat down in the chair next to Summer.

She could feel her cheeks going red. Had he heard any of the previous conversation? From his relaxed reaction, it didn't seem as though he had. She straightened in her chair and pasted a smile in place. 'Tough meeting?' she asked, as Alyssa headed off to make herself a cup of coffee.

'They wouldn't stop talking.' Jason slumped forward onto the desk and put his head down.

'You look exhausted.'

'I'm feeling it.'

'Just as well I'm doing the weekend shift. You can put your feet up and relax, Dr Daniels.'

He lifted his head then and looked at her. 'Yeah. I guess I can and not worry that a know-it-all Melbournian locum is going to change all departmental policies by the time I return on Monday.'

Summer laughed. 'Was it really that bad?'

He wished she wouldn't laugh. She really was far too appealing when she did that. 'Felt like it sometimes. What's Tommy doing for the weekend?'

'He's spending most of it with Bradley. Having his first ever sleep-over on Saturday night.'

'He's never had a sleep-over before?'

'No. I told you he was always quite reserved.'

'What? Even with his friends?'

'Yes.' She felt bad saying that her son hadn't had any real friends. The boys he'd talked to at school had been the same ones he'd spent time with at charity affairs and parties. Those boys were the offspring of the Sydney social set and were all as self-centred as their parents.

'What about camping?'

'Camping?' Summer looked at him as though the word were completely foreign.

'You know. Outdoors. Tent. Campfire. Sleeping bags. Wrap it all up into a swag and carry it on your back as you hike through the bush.'

'A swag?'

Jason shook his head and threw his hands up in the air in disgust. 'You've never carried a swag? What sort of Australians are you?'

'We be city dwellers,' she replied with a laugh.

'I can see, Dr Hoyts, that there are some gaping holes in your small-town education. Sure, you've moved here, made new friends and settled into life quite nicely, but to never have been camping?' He tut-tutted. 'I think we might need to rectify this.'

'You're going to take me camping?' She was utterly astounded.

'You and Tommy. Sure.'

'Really?'

'Something strange about that? After all, you did want a new life with new experiences. I think camping would definitely classify as a new experience.'

Summer decided he was probably just being polite and really meant nothing by the invitation so she decided to laugh it off, as she had with Rhonda and Alyssa earlier. 'So long as wherever we camp has a very comfortable mattress, hot running water, a fully functional bathroom and room service, I'll gladly carry a swag and sleep in a sleeping bag.'

Jason laughed. Never had he enjoyed a woman's conversation as much as he enjoyed Summer's. True to his resolution, he'd made friends with Summer and kept his distance as far as the attraction between them went. They'd seen each other a few times in their apartment complex but it had usually been as one of them had been going out and the other coming in.

The odd thing was that the more he got to know Summer, the more they chatted about non-specific things, about life in general and nothing on a deeply personal level, the more he wanted to dig a little deeper. It was as though he now needed to prove to himself that she was exactly like Amanda because the sooner he realised that, the sooner he'd be able to get his life back on track.

Still, he'd found himself watching her every now and then, hopefully when she'd been unaware of his presence. If she ever caught him, he'd probably blush beetroot red and he'd *never* blushed before in his life. Just now he'd stopped himself at the doorway into the ward, watching as she'd talked and joked with Rhonda and Alyssa, presumably about the upcoming hospital ball. He hadn't been able to hear exactly what they'd been saying but it had seemed to be the top pick topic of conversation for every woman in the hospital of late. He'd also noticed that as the two nurses had chatted on, Summer had sat there, staring into space,

and instinctively he'd known she'd been thinking about something in her past.

It was an odd sensation, to be sure of what
someone else was thinking, and he'd never felt
it before. It was as though he was in tune with
her, and where at first he'd felt like running
from the sensation, he was now quite intrigued
by it.

'That might take a bit of extra planning,' he
remarked about her criteria.

'Then go to it, man. Don't let me keep you.
Might even give you something to think about
on your weekend off.'

Jason smiled. 'I was planning on catching up
on my reading but this sounds like a project I
could really sink my teeth into.'

Summer eyed him sceptically for a moment. 'I
wasn't really being serious, Jason. You don't need
to worry about taking Tommy and I camping.'

'I beg to differ.' Now that the idea had been
voiced, he wanted to carry it through. Camping
was so real, so raw that it always showed a
person's true nature. 'It's important that you experience it at least once.'

'Or not.'

'It'll be good for Tommy.'

'How do you know?'

'Because I'm a guy. Guys need to get outside in the wilderness. It's a throwback to the caveman days,' he pointed out, as though that explained everything. 'We need to get back to nature. Breathe the fresh air. Hit the open road.'

'Beat your chests?'

'Exactly.'

'Well, I can breathe fresh air and hit the road simply by walking outside the hospital.'

Jason smiled at her. 'Now you're being funny.'

'I try my hardest.'

'I think an overnight camp would be good for Tommy and his mother, or are you too much of a princess to accept the challenge?' Jason wasn't sure why he was pressing her so hard to agree to this. His first rationalisation was that he was only being friendly, neighbourly. He'd do the same for anyone else in the hospital who wanted to try camping for the first time.

His second rationalisation was that spending some extra time with Summer away from the hospital, away from everyone else and putting her in a different setting, would help to bring out her flaws. It was a way to almost prove to himself that she wasn't all she appeared to be. That he'd find deeper layers and that those layers would reveal her true self.

It had happened with Amanda and he'd long since wished he'd dug a little deeper before he'd asked her to marry him. Not that he was planning to marry Summer. No. Marriage to any woman wasn't in his future plans because when it came to love, he didn't trust any woman as far as he could throw her. However, a camping trip would help little Tommy, so it should all be worth it. Right?

'A challenge?'

'Are you the type of woman to back down from a challenge?'

Her eyes twinkled with determination and humour. 'Not any more.'

'So you think you'd be able to handle it?'

'If I can handle the inner Sydney set of bitchy socialites, I think I can handle anything.'

'Hmm. One jungle to another.'

'Exactly.'

Jason held out his hand and watched as Summer put hers instantly into it. They shook, both ignoring the sparks that zinged around their bodies at the touch. It was the first time he'd ventured to touch her in two weeks and it was as though those weeks had produced a drought because this time when they came into contact, it somehow seemed to be more powerful than previous.

'You're on.'

'It's a deal.' They spoke together. 'I'll make the arrangements, make sure it's on a weekend we're both rostered off and get back to you.'

'And you'll remember my criteria?'

'Comfortable mattress, bathroom, room service.'

'You forgot hot running water.'

'Right. Right. Got it.'

'OK. I'll figure out a way to break the news to my son.'

At the mention of Tommy, Jason grinned. 'He's gonna love it.'

That night, as she was getting ready for bed, Summer thought back over her conversation with Jason, still astonished that what had started out as a throw-away comment had ended up with the promise of a camping trip. A camping trip with a man who still kept invading her dreams every night, no matter how hard she tried to banish him.

After checking that Tommy was sleeping peacefully, she went into the bathroom and brushed her teeth, taking her hair down from the style she always wore to work, the blond tresses falling about her shoulders. She looked at herself in the mirror, being critical of her looks. Her eyes, she'd always thought, were a little too close together and her nose seemed too straight sometimes. Of course, she'd been the envy of the social set because she hadn't needed to have any cosmetic surgery done. Summer shook her head, glad those days were now behind her.

She headed back to her bedroom and changed into her satin pink pyjamas before resolving to tackle the very last packing box which stood over in the corner of the room. It was the box that contained her wedding photographs and other memorabilia of her life with Cameron. She'd left the box to last because she wasn't quite sure where she should put its contents.

After discovering what she had about the secret life of her husband since his death, she hadn't even been able to *look* at her wedding pictures, now knowing what a farce her marriage had been.

She knew Cameron had been having an affair, especially considering he hadn't touched her since Tommy's birth. It was as though he'd done his duty, provided an heir to the Hoyts fortune, and that he had then been free to resume his playboy lifestyle. The little woman had no longer mattered. That had hurt. The fact that her own husband hadn't found her attractive had definitely hurt and although they'd smiled and continued to attend functions as a couple, it had all been completely fake.

She realised that her attraction to Jason had also been fuelled due to the fact that he wasn't at all immune to her charms. She knew he definitely found her appealing because of the looks they'd shared. It was so exciting that she knew that was half the reason why it was increasingly difficult *not* to think about him. A man who really thought she was attractive. Someone who liked her for who she was both inside and out—

not because she looked pretty on his arm and came complete with her own family fortune.

Summer stared at the box and shook her head. 'You can do this. You can unpack this box. You're bigger than this and it's only photographs. You're keeping them for Tommy's sake, not yours, so just put them away on the top shelf where they can gather dust and you can forget about them.' With her pep talk done, she took a deep breath and opened the box. She took out something rectangular wrapped in white butcher's paper, only to discover it was the gilded frame that contained her wedding picture.

She looked down at her smiling image, recalling how happy she'd been on that day. Finally, she'd told herself, she'd found a place to belong. She'd been floundering in a sea of confusion ever since her parents had died during her final year at medical school, leaving her all alone except for a few distant cousins who lived overseas and whom she barely knew.

Three years later, she'd met Cameron and he'd swept her off her feet, courting and wooing her and making her fall in love with him. He'd encouraged her to continue her paediatric training, only asking that after they were married she work part time only. She'd been more than happy to do as he'd asked, filling the rest of her time with charity work and social functions organised by his mother.

'The Hoyts family name is highly esteemed and as such you must be beyond reproach,' Cameron's mother had often told her, usually when Summer had made a blunder.

Summer put the photograph down on the bed, pushing the thoughts away. The Hoyts family were in her past and there wasn't anything she could do to change it. Walking to the box, she took another wrapped parcel out and discovered it was Cameron's family bible, something she hadn't taken much interest in but it had meant the world to him. It contained lists of generations of Hoyts men and one day the book might be of interest to Tommy, if he chose that life. As she turned it over in her hand, she felt something touch her lightly.

Her eyes widened as the long brown leg of a spider touched her again. Screaming, she threw the book onto the floor and ran from the room, shuddering all the way. She hated spiders. Ridiculous, she knew, given that she was far taller and bigger than them, but still... She shuddered again, her heart pounding in her chest.

Quickly, she checked on Tommy in case she'd woken him but he slept on. She was further startled by a loud knocking at her front door.

'Summer?'

She rushed towards the door and flung it open. Without waiting for an invitation, Jason walked past her and looked quickly about the room.

'What happened? I heard you scream. Are you all right? Is it Tommy? Are you—' He stopped as his eyes settled on her. His jaw dropped and his mouth dried as he simply stood there and stared at her. He pointed, then dropped his hand back to his side.

'Your hair.' It was loose. It was flowing freely around her shoulders, framing her face as he'd often pictured it would. 'You're...stunning.'

CHAPTER FOUR

THE spider. The unpacking. The memories.

It all disappeared into thin air as Summer stood there in her pyjamas, staring at Jason. He was dressed only in a pair of jeans that looked as though they'd long forgotten any shape but his own. His bare chest was firm, rippled with contours that her fingers itched to touch.

It had been a long time, longer than anyone would have suspected, since she'd seen a man in such a state of undress, and her heart started to pound out a wild rhythm against her rib cage. He didn't say a word but continued to stare at her, his last two words still ringing in her ears.

He thought she was stunning? How could that be? She was about to get into bed and go to sleep. She was wearing comfortable but old pyjamas and had no make-up on. She hadn't even brushed her hair after taking it down—

instead, she'd sifted her fingers through the locks, giving her scalp a bit of a massage. How could he think she looked stunning?

'J-Jason.' His name was a whisper as she dragged her gaze away from his naked torso to finally look into his rich, brown eyes. The desire, the attraction she'd seen there before had now intensified and she knew it was going to take all the willpower in the world to get through the next few minutes. 'I'm…I'm… fi—'

'Stunning,' he said again, and took a step towards her. When he'd arrived home from the hospital that evening, he'd managed to convince himself the camping trip was nothing but a friendly way to help Summer out with Tommy. They were colleagues. Neighbours. Possibly, you could even call them friends. Nothing more.

Until he'd heard her scream.

As the sound had pierced the air, Jason had felt the blood drain from his body, his eyes staring intently towards his front door, every nerve ending telling him to move, to check she was all right. With his heart pounding wildly, his mind whirring through several scenarios as to what might have happened to make her scream, Jason had instantly stalked over, wishing he'd thought to trade keys with her—purely for an incident such as this.

What if the apartment was about to catch fire? What if Tommy was hurt? If he'd fallen and split his head open? What if a burglar had crashed through her living-room window? What if she was in mortal danger? What if she was hurt?

He'd pounded on the door. His heart hammering as fast as his mind was sifting through what he might find on the other side of the door. And then…she'd opened it. And she'd looked… stunning.

Whatever resolutions he'd made, whatever speeches he'd given, whatever else he'd done to trick himself into thinking nothing existed between them, that there was no reciprocal attraction, were completely useless. It wasn't a question, it wasn't a debate, it was a fact. Summer was stunning.

'No.' She held up both hands. 'Don't.' Closing her eyes, she shook her head. 'Please, don't.' When she opened them, it was to find he'd shoved his hands into his pockets.

'Don't what?'

'Look at me the way you're looking at me.'

'Why not? You're looking at me in much the same way.'

'I know. I'm sorry. I'm so sorry.' Summer still didn't seem able to move from the spot where she stood. 'I'm fine.'

'You screamed.'

'I know. I'm sorry,' she repeated. 'I didn't mean to disturb you.'

Jason took another step closer and this time Summer found she could move and shifted backwards. 'You've been disturbing me since we first met.' His voice was rich, was full of raw, honest emotion.

'I have?' The words rushed out on a breath of pure excitement. No man had ever spoken to her in such an open and honest way before and she found it incredibly powerful and highly addictive.

'Yes. Oh, yes.' He came closer and this time, when she stepped back, she found herself against the wall. Jason continued towards her, only stopping when he was standing so close she could feel the warmth radiating from his body. He was so near, creating such havoc with her equilibrium, that her palms started to perspire.

'Uh…well, I'm sorry. I didn't mean to.'

'Don't apologise.'

With her eyes fixed on his, her lips parted to allow the pent-up air to escape as her breathing continued at the rate of knots.

'Because it also appears that I have an equal reaction on you,' he continued.

'Yes.' The word was whispered without hesitation.

'You're not scared of me?'

'No. Not of you but of the way you make me feel.'

'Because you don't want to feel that way?'

'Correct.'

'Me neither.'

Summer swallowed and knew she either needed to get some much-needed distance between them or to throw caution and common sense completely to the wind and close the distance between them.

'Yet we do,' she continued. 'Jason, I'm just not ready for—'

'Shh.' He placed a warm finger over her lips

and Summer thought she would come apart, every nerve ending in her body ready to explode. 'I understand.'

'You do?' Her words were now barely audible but she knew Jason could hear her. It was as though in that moment their hearts and their minds were completely connected and that had never happened to her before.

'Yes.'

'That makes one of us.'

'Neither of us asked for this thing between us, Summer, but it's there.'

'What do we do?'

Jason's eyes flicked down to her lips, looking at the rich fullness, the sweetness he knew he was only a breath away from tasting. If he leaned forward, if he did what he'd been wanting to do for weeks now, and pressed his lips to hers, he knew she wouldn't fight him. He also knew that the instant he did that, he wouldn't be able to stop. So powerful was the pull towards her that for the first time since Amanda had ripped his heart out and torn it into a million little pieces, Jason had the desire to risk it all again, to gamble with the one thing that had torn his life apart before, and if he wasn't careful could tear his life apart again. Was he that strong? Could he resist Summer?

He had to. For both their sakes.

Still looking at her lips, he dragged air into his lungs and forced himself to take a giant step backwards. 'Nothing.' His eyes met hers and he could see both relief combined with immense disappointment welling up within her.

'Nothing?' she repeated. Why, although she knew it was completely and utterly the right thing to do, did that knowledge make her suddenly feel so sad?

'We can't, Summer.'

She nodded, knowing he spoke the truth. 'No. We can't.'

'I've had one failed marriage and from the few things you've said it's clear you've been through your own problems since your husband's death. The attraction is definitely there but the timing isn't. If it was a few more years down the track, if things were more settled for both of us then…' He stopped, forcing himself not to look at her luscious lips. 'I don't want to hurt you, Summer, and although that may sound self-sacrificing, it isn't, because I also don't want to get hurt. Not again.'

'That's fair enough.' Somehow, from somewhere, rational thought was starting to return and if he kept his distance, they might actually be able to get through this. Summer held her hands firmly together in an effort to stop herself from fidgeting. 'Your wife really pulled you apart?'

'Inside out,' he confirmed.

'I'm sorry, Jason.'

He took his hand from his pocket and raked it through his hair. 'We live, we learn, we grow up.' We vow never to go down that path again, he added silently, as though trying to bring himself back into line.

'Yes, we do, although some days I really wish I could let go. You know, be like I used to be back in med school before I was forced to grow up.'

A slow smile spread over Jason's face. 'Exactly. My life before I met Amanda seemed to be filled with…' He shrugged. 'I don't know.'

'Contentment?'

'I suppose so, yes. I had confidence in myself on a personal level. When I met Amanda and realised she was interested in me, I was surprised.'

'Why?'

His smile increased and he shook his head. 'I keep forgetting you're not from around these parts and therefore don't know the story.'

'Will you tell me?'

'There isn't much to tell. Amanda was a model. *Is* still a model. A very successful one now but back then she was just starting out. Small things at first. She entered beauty pageants. She was crowned Miss Ballarat three years in a row.'

'Three years? Impressive.'

'For her, yes. She started getting some modelling work in Melbourne just before we got engaged. Afterwards, she encouraged me to apply for a job at the Melbourne Children's Hospital and so we lived in the city for most of our married life. She modelled. I worked long hours in the paediatric unit there but my heart was back here in Ballarat.' He shrugged again. 'When she announced she'd been offered work overseas, I just wasn't interested. That's about it, really. We seemed to spend less and less time together and grew apart.'

She could clearly tell that wasn't all. There was definitely more to the story but tonight that was all he was going to give. 'Absence sometimes doesn't make the heart grow fonder.'

'You say that as though you mean it.'

'I do.'

Jason shifted, knowing he was about to cross that invisible line once more. 'Summer, I take it your marriage wasn't all that happy?'

'It was at first as I think all marriages are, otherwise why would you do it? Then things start to go wrong. People change or you find out the truth about them. I don't know. I guess it was that Cameron needed me to be a certain sort of person and because I loved him I did my best. He worked long hours at the hospital, had a hand in the family business, which his father still ran, and was heavily involved in charity events, largely sponsored by his family.'

Jason frowned for a moment. 'Family?' Then his eyes widened and his jaw dropped. 'Hoyts. Your surname is Hoyts!'

'You knew that.'

'You belong to *the* Hoyts family?'

'Belonged. Past tense.'

'They practically own Sydney. Heavily into property, the stock markets, supporting local businesses and raising millions for charity.' He whistled. 'They do good work.'

'I'm not denying that.'

'Ah.' A lightbulb went on in his mind. 'You were required to change in order to fit in with the family image.'

'To an extent, yes.'

'Which is why you dress the way you do.'

Summer gave him a puzzled smile. 'Do I dress a certain way?' She indicated her pyjamas.

'You dress…' As his gaze washed over her, he felt the same tightening in his gut which he'd only just managed to relax. He took a step back. 'You dress impeccably and everything you wear looks amazing on you.' He looked away and raked both hands through his hair.

'I'm wearing my oldest pyjamas.'

'And I've already told you that you look stunning.' Her big blue eyes, her loose, flowing blond hair, her lithe body. In that moment Jason realised he could be in real trouble if he stayed. He cleared his throat. 'Uh…and this is where we came in.'

'Hmm?' It took another second for her mind to clear from the way he'd been looking at her again. 'Oh, right. I screamed. You almost broke down my door and then... Yes. This is where we came in.'

'Why *did* you scream? I guess as I came over here to rescue you, I should at least find out why.'

'True. Uh...spider.'

'I'll get it for you.'

'It's...uh...in my...bedroom.'

'Bedroom?' That was the one room in her apartment he knew he should avoid but he'd come over here to play the hero and play the hero he would just as long as she kept her distance. 'We can't have you sleeping with a spider crawling around in your room. Whereabouts was it?'

Summer started to head towards her room to show him but he stopped her.

'Just *tell* me where it is or was. You don't need to show me.' Because they didn't need to be alone in *that* room. Where the bed was. Where she slept.

'Oh. All right. Well, it should be somewhere around the packing box. It's the last box and I thought I'd just get it unpacked before bed and when I took out a book it was on it and…' She shuddered and started brushing off her shoulders as though it might be on there.

'Right. Well, before you start doing the spider-slap-dance, as my sister used to, I'll go get it. Can you get me a glass and piece of paper or something I can slide beneath the glass?'

'Sure.' Summer quickly went into the kitchen and retrieved what he needed then headed to her room. She saw Jason standing at the foot of her bed, looking down at the wedding picture she'd tossed there. What did he see when he looked at that photograph? All Summer saw were broken promises and a life built on lies. 'Jason?'

'Hmm?' He turned, a guilty look flitting across his face before he came and took the items from her. He pointed to the photograph. 'You look happy.'

'I was and then I wasn't. I didn't know what to do with the photographs and family things but I owe it to Tommy to keep them and—'

'It's OK. You don't need to explain. We both have pasts.' He held up the paper and the glass. 'Thanks. Now be very, very quiet. I'm hunting spiders.' He winked at her and in that instant

Summer felt as though a huge weight had been lifted off her shoulders. She couldn't explain why but it was as though she knew no matter how much she and Jason had just shared about their past hurts or no matter how intent they were on ignoring the mounting attraction between them, the new friendship they'd somehow managed to forge was going to survive and that, in itself, meant the world to her.

Summer worked through the weekend, enjoying the different pace. She was required in A and E for quite a few consults because the town was definitely getting into the Christmas cheer. This week's event for the Twelve Weeks of Christmas was a bike ride through the city and then around Lake Wendouree with the general community getting involved.

She saw two boys who had fractured their arms after falls from their bikes, treated several patients for cuts and minor abrasions, admitted one eleven-year-old girl who was suffering from dehydration and treated a completely unrelated case of a toddler getting into the medicine cabinet and drinking a bottle of paracetamol. Thankfully, activated charcoal did the trick but Summer wanted the child admitted overnight for observation.

'You certainly had a busy time of it on the weekend,' Jason commented when he read through the reports for the past few days.

'Yes. Brilliant introduction to the weekend shift, I thought.'

'I'll bet you're used to handling three times as many cases with your hands tied behind your back while hopping up and down on one leg whistling "Dixie".'

Summer smiled. 'Actually, I whistle the tune to "Timbuktu" but close enough.'

Jason laughed, simply enjoying being with her. He knew they couldn't do anything about the attraction they felt towards each other, and openly admitting it to each other had actually helped to take a bit of pressure off his shoulders. However, he'd definitely found himself thinking about her even more after he'd removed the spider from her apartment on Friday evening.

He no longer needed to wonder what she looked like with her hair down. He no longer needed to wonder what she looked like before she went to bed. He no longer needed to wonder what it would be like to be so close to her he could feel her tremble.

Those thoughts alone had been his constant companions over the weekend, and while he'd been spending time with his sister, Cassandra, he'd often found his thoughts turning to Summer. Several times he'd convinced himself he could just idly drop into the hospital to see how she was doing, under the pretence of having paperwork to complete, but he'd held himself in check and kept away. His distractedness, however, hadn't escaped his sister's notice and he'd had to work hard to successfully evade her probing questions.

'So, how did Tommy's sleep-over at Bradley's go?'

'Very well.'

'He survived? You didn't have to go and pick him up at eleven o'clock in the evening?'

'No. He did very well and is extremely proud of himself.'

'He has every right to be. And what about Bradley? How's he coping?' He knew Summer would have taken the opportunity to watch their young patient, to see how he was coping in his home environment with the eye patching he would require for quite a few months.

'Very well. His vision was tracking perfectly when I went to pick up Tommy and he seems to be coping well with the lack of depth perception. Of course, Tommy had a patch over his eye, too, and both of them were busy playing pirates.'

Jason's grin was wide. 'Any excuse will do. That's an excellent report.'

'Thank you. Oh, and I did receive a call on Sunday afternoon from Katy's parents. Apparently she banged her head on the dining-room table. They couldn't see any damage and although Katy was a little upset when it happened, she soon quietened down, but I still thought it best if she was reviewed. They brought her in, everything looks fine, but they want you to put their minds at rest because they trust you.'

'OK. That doesn't bother you at all? Them wanting a second opinion from me?'

'Not at all. As parents, they need to be confident their daughter is healthy and if you're the person they'll listen to most, go to it.'

Jason only nodded. He knew it was because Summer was a mother that she understood these sorts of things. 'I presume you've added her to the clinic list?'

'I have indeed.'

'Good. Thank you, Dr Hoyts.'

'You're welcome, Dr Daniels.'

They sat at the nurses' station, simply smiling at each other for a few seconds.

'Well. I have meetings,' Jason said, breaking eye contact as he picked up a batch of papers to take with him. He wasn't two steps away from the desk before he stopped and turned back. 'Summer, I keep forgetting to ask if you're going to be free this Saturday.'

'This Saturday?' Her heart began to hammer. Why did he want to know if she was free? Was he going to ask her out? She wasn't sure what to do as she thought they'd agreed that they were simply going to be friends and now he was asking her whether or not she was free on Saturday.

'Tommy, too, if he's not at Bradley's again.'

'Tommy, too?'

'Is there an echo?' He laughed. 'It's nothing major except that this hospital provides a home-care service, mainly for those patients who require a bit of extra follow-up after their discharge. Doctors are rostered on from all departments and this weekend is my turn. You won't be on until after Christmas but I thought if you wanted to tag along with me, see what the protocols and procedures are, it might be fun.'

'To go on house calls?' She'd done the odd house call in Sydney and it hadn't been fun in any way, shape or form.

'Sure.'

'And you want me to bring Tommy?'

'I think he'd enjoy it. He'd get to meet a few more people, see a bit more of the area.' And *he* would be able to spend time with the seven-year-old. From what he'd seen of Tommy, he was a quiet boy who was very wary of people. Jason liked kids but he also liked to find out what made each one tick. He'd found that in doing so it had helped him numerous times when it came to treating his patients. Tommy also seemed…a bit broken, for want of a better word, and that alone intrigued him. Besides, he and Summer were friends and for that reason he wanted to get to know her son a bit better. 'So what do you say?'

Summer thought for a moment and knew that if Jason said it was going to be fun, then it was probably because *he* made it fun. He seemed to have a knack for turning mundane tasks into an adventure. 'OK.'

'Excellent. I'll come and knock on your door around seven.'

She raised her eyes at the early starting time, especially as it was supposed to be her day off.

'We need to get an early start.' He shrugged apologetically. 'Lots of ground to cover. I'll provide breakfast. There's a terrific bakery in town.' He kissed his fingers. 'The best croissants I've ever tasted—except for those actually made in France. Nothing in the world can beat those but these come pretty close.'

'Wow. Sounds like something I should experience.'

'It is.' He shifted his files, knowing he should simply smile and walk away, but there was something about this woman, something that kept drawing him in every time he told himself to walk away. He didn't have a clue what it was but he knew it was there and he knew he was having a difficult time fighting it. 'Do you really like experiencing new things?'

The words came out in a softer, deeper tone and Jason swallowed, hoping she didn't think he was trying it on as a pick-up line—which he belatedly realised was exactly the way it had sounded.

'I never used to. Same old, same old was the way I lived my life for the past decade.'

'And now?'

'I'm here, aren't I? New challenges. New experiences. That's what I'm trying to do.'

'True. So, I guess you *do* like new experiences.'

She nodded. 'Especially culinary ones. Tommy likes croissants as well,' she pointed out, hoping the mention of her son would help them to stop having the underlying conversation with their eyes and focus on the words they were saying.

'It's all good, then.' He smiled. 'Now, I'd better get going before I'm late.'

'Oh, Jason. Before you go. I keep forgetting

to ask someone. When do the Christmas decorations usually go up? Some of the children have been asking and given that it's now November...' She spread her arms wide.

'Good question. We start making them right about now.'

'Making?'

'Yes.'

'You *make* the decorations?'

'Most of them, yeah. The children help.' At the astonished look on her face Jason realised she'd never been involved in such a simple task before. 'We usually do it in the playroom and we have lots of coloured paper and scissors and pasting and glitter. Oh, the glitter. The cleaning staff hate it because they can never get it all vacuumed up.'

'Glitter?' She said the word slowly, as though trying to figure out just what it was.

Jason couldn't help but smile. 'Sparkly stuff you use to decorate things with.'

'I know what glitter is but doesn't it then drop all around the ward?'

His tone had dropped a level and a teasing gleam had entered his eyes. 'Which is why the cleaning staff hate it but, believe me, we use it with the utmost care and only for the best of the best of the *best* decorations—which is usually all of them. They'll be doing stuff after school, too, so bring Tommy along. He'll love it.'

'Another new experience for me?'

He leaned towards her as he spoke and she instantly felt a heat wash over her at his nearness. 'It looks as though you're going to be having quite a few new experiences, Summer, and I'm more than happy to help you through each and every one.'

CHAPTER FIVE

ON SATURDAY morning, Summer and Tommy were up, dressed and ready bright and early, waiting for the knock on their door which would herald Jason's arrival.

'Why can't I go to Bradley's?' Tommy asked his mother.

'We've been over this.' Summer checked her appearance in the mirror. She'd decided to take a chance today and change her hairstyle from her usual clipped-back style. Jason had reacted with such abandonment when he'd seen it loose last week, when he'd come over to play her knight in shining armour, that it was with that thought alone she'd decided to try something different.

It wasn't all down, it would totally get in her way, but instead she'd used a pearl-encrusted clip to pull her hair half up, half down. Was it too much? Would it distract Jason? Was that what she wanted? Every single night this week she'd gone to bed thinking about him, wondering what he was doing, wondering what would happen tomorrow.

At the hospital they were still behaving in a friendly manner and Summer was pleased that they seemed to think alike on a lot of structural and procedural matters as far as the department went. Their patient care was also very similar and to that end they were able to back each other up when needed and offer support if it was required.

Never before had she felt so comfortable at work, not only because of Jason but because of all of the staff. Alyssa and Rhonda had invited her to join them for coffee after their shift had finished the other day and the three of them had had a wonderful time. Prior to her move to Ballarat, Summer's friends had been the wives of Cameron's friends. She'd liked them but a lot of the time she hadn't necessarily understood them and now, reflecting back on her life of the past decade, it was starting to feel as though that life had been someone else's.

'I think I hear him,' Tommy whispered, his ear pressed to the front door.

'Come away from there,' Summer said with a laugh. 'Or he'll knock so loudly it'll damage your eardrum.'

'Really?' Tommy was astounded.

Summer laughed again. 'No. Not really. I was exaggerating.'

Tommy straightened up but didn't move away from the door. Instead, he gave his mother a quizzical look. 'You laugh a lot now.'

'What?' Her smile increased at his words.

'Since we came here. You laugh. You never used to laugh like this back in Sydney.'

Summer swooped forward and gathered her son up, spinning him around the room while she hugged him close.

'You're insane.' Tommy giggled and the sound was like music to her ears. She stopped spinning, both of them collapsing onto the lounge.

'You're right, darling. I do laugh more.'

'It's nice.' His words were said easily, with the sweet and innocent acceptance of a child. Tommy didn't snuggle into her but he also didn't try to get away as he usually did when she let loose with outward displays of affection.

'It is,' she agreed.

When the knock at the door came, Tommy was up and had the door open before she could straighten herself.

'Caught you at a bad moment?' Jason asked as he took in Summer sprawled out on the lounge.

'Mummy was spinning me around,' Tommy said, his eyes still wide at his mother's uncharacteristic behaviour.

'Oh, well. No wonder she's still loafing about.'

'I beg your pardon,' Summer said as she stood and gathered her things together. 'I do not loaf about.'

'Looked that way to me,' Jason teased with a wink. 'Shall we?' He stepped back into the hallway, needing a few seconds to simply get over the sight of how incredible Summer looked. Today she was dressed in a pair of black trousers and a pale pink top which was cut in an oriental style and buttoned down the front. Her hypnotic scent had sent his senses into hyperdrive the instant Tommy had opened the door and he'd seen her lying back amongst the cushions, a smile on her luscious lips and her eyes alive with merriment.

She came out after her son, locking the door behind her before they went outside. Jason led them over to a red Jaguar and received a gulp of astonished approval from Tommy.

'This is *your* car?'

'Yep.'

'I told Brad that there was a cool car at our building but I didn't know it was *yours*!'

'And that's all you need to do to win a seven-year-old boy's heart,' Summer said softly as Jason held the passenger door open for her.

It was on the tip of his tongue to ask her what he needed to do to win over a thirty-five-year-old, sexy paediatrician's heart, but he caught himself just in time. They were friends and he was discovering that he had to keep reminding himself of that every moment they spent together.

They were soon on their way, with Jason explaining, more for Tommy's sake, what they'd be doing that day. They stopped at a bakery in town where the croissants not only lived up to Jason's promise but the bakery also had the most delicious hot chocolate to accompany the pastries.

'We're going to be visiting some great people,' Jason told Tommy as they finished off their breakfast. 'Just relax, OK? Be yourself and have a bit of fun.'

'I'm used to visiting sick people.' Tommy's tone was now as bland as it had been earlier when he'd kept asking Summer why he needed to go.

'You are?'

'Tommy's been involved with the Hoyts family's charity work since he was small,' Summer pointed out.

'Ah. Of course. I'd temporarily forgotten.' Forgotten that Summer had previously come from another world—the world of the rich, and no doubt, famous, too. 'Well…I still hope you enjoy yourself.'

Summer looked over the list Jason had handed her and was surprised they'd be seeing at least twenty different people today. Thank goodness Ballarat wasn't all that big and it shouldn't take them too long to get from one place to the next.

'What are the ones marked in blue?'

'They're the new ones for this week.'

'There's only five of them. Do you mean

everyone else on this list gets a visit once a week from a member of the medical staff?'

Jason wasn't sure whether she was disgusted or delighted. 'I mean exactly that. Sometimes it's more. Some people only need fortnightly visits and, of course, there's the district nurses, who usually go and see most of these house-bound people once, even twice during the week, sometimes every day if necessary.'

'That's amazing. It's wonderful that the hospital has such a fantastic programme.'

It wasn't far to their first house call and they all bundled out of the car. Jason noticed Tommy almost slip on a game face—his best manners, no doubt—as they walked up the front steps of the old weatherboard house. 'Mr and Mrs Calvin's house. She and her husband are house-bound because of their failing respiratory health. We're trying to keep them at their home together for as long as we possibly can.' He knocked on the door, then opened it and walked right in, calling out a greeting as he went. Tommy's eyes went big at the action and Summer couldn't help but smile. 'They used to be entertainers,' Jason said quietly as Mrs Calvin answered them.

'In here, dear. You're nice and early. Just the way I like you. Ooh, and, look, Josiah, he's brought us visitors.' Mrs Calvin beckoned them in and laughed when Tommy just stood there, staring around the room. She coughed a few times but it didn't deter her jovial spirits. 'Come in, come in, young man. Have a look at anything you want.'

The room was covered—almost wall to wall—with photographs. Some in colour, a lot in black and white and in all of them there were smiling, happy faces. None of the photographs had been framed and Summer realised, as she leaned a little closer to take a look at a young woman who she suspected was Mrs Calvin over fifty years ago, that they were actually stuck to the wall. The room was done in découpage style.

'Who's that?' Tommy asked, his tone filled with awe and wonderment. He was pointing to a black-and-white photograph of a man wearing clown make-up and a top hat. There was a large feather coming out of the hat and on top of the picture a real large, red feather had been stuck onto the wall over the photograph, making it three-dimensional.

'That's me,' Josiah wheezed, an oxygen

cylinder close at hand. 'I'd just come off stage after seven curtain calls.'

Mrs Calvin clutched her hands together. 'It was a wonderful night. That was at Christmas time.' Mrs Calvin was more than happy to tell Tommy stories attached to the different photographs while Summer and Jason started with Josiah's check-up. Suffering from emphysema, he was now paying the price for a lifetime of smoking but he wasn't at all bitter.

'We've had a good life,' he wheezed. 'And we can sit here and look at the pictures on the wall and remember.'

'And if we don't remember,' Mrs Calvin interjected, 'we just make it up, don't we, Jos?' She didn't wait for him to answer but instead took Tommy over to the other side of the wall and showed him another picture.

Jason was happy with Josiah's status and so the two patients switched roles and while Summer listened to Mrs Calvin's heart and lungs, ensuring her asthma was being correctly treated, Josiah told Tommy a few more tales, her son listening intently even though it took Josiah quite a while to get his rasping words out. He would place the oxygen mask over his mouth and nose every now and then, breathe deeply and then go on. It didn't seem to faze Tommy at all, he was far too interested in the story.

'They were *awesome*,' the seven-year-old announced as they left the Calvins' house. 'That room. Mum, did you see that room?'

'I saw it.'

'Can I do my room like that?'

Summer turned around to look at him. 'Um…how about you start by collecting photographs first? You have to remember that the Calvins have over fifty years of pictures on their walls.'

'So when I'm like thirty, can I do it then?'

Jason smiled as he drove the car, waiting for Summer's reply.

'I think there's a definite possibility,' she replied with all seriousness.

'Totally buzzin',' he replied, and sat back, no doubt picturing his room in their apartment covered in photographs.

The next two house calls weren't nearly as exciting as Summer and Jason changed the dressing on old Mr Peterson's ulcerated leg and then saw Mr Fu who had not long returned from Melbourne, having received a new artificial leg.

'I lost a leg when I was mining for gold. I was only twenty-two,' he told Tommy. Mr Fu was standing perfectly on his new prosthesis in the kitchen, cooking sweet dumplings. 'You stay. You eat. My family make dumplings for many generations.'

While they ate, Jason asked Mr Fu questions about the new leg, impressed with the leaps and bounds in orthotic prostheses. 'And you have almost full range of motion?'

Mr Fu demonstrated exactly what he could do with his new leg, running up and down the corridor. It made Tommy giggle and Mr Fu joined in.

'What a range of characters you have in this town,' Summer remarked as they headed north-west. 'And how generous of him to give us some dumplings to take home.'

'Just you wait. Sometimes you get quite a haul of food when you do house calls. People are so grateful for the time and effort and that's one small way they can say thank you. Personally, though, Mr Fu's sweet dumplings are a favourite of mine.'

'Where are we going now?' Summer looked at their surroundings, which had quickly changed to a definite rural feel as Jason took the freeway out of Ballarat. As they drove along, she and Tommy gasped in delight as they saw emus running around, one coming up to have a race with them along the fence line.

'We have several calls out here. People mainly need the house calls because of their isolation or being unable to make it to clinics due to farming pressures.' He pointed to the list. 'And I hope you both enjoy Monica's.'

'Why? What's Monica's? Is that a person or a place?' Tommy asked, now completely intrigued with his day. 'Hey, Mum, when it's your real turn to do house calls, can I come with you? I want to see the Calvins again and Mr Fu's dumplings are the best.'

Her eyebrows hit her hairline at the request. 'Uh...I don't see why not.'

'Totally buzzin'. Wait till I tell Brad about today. He's gonna choke.'

Summer smiled at the way her son was talking. Even his speech was more relaxed than usual and that small thing made her happy. They continued with their list, Tommy always asking when they'd finally get to Monica's house so he could find out why Jason thought it would be good. Finally, when Jason drove the car up a long, dirt driveway of a farm that had been heavily stricken by the drought, he told them Monica's story.

'Monica was born with many birth defects. She had a hole in her heart, had surgery the day after she was born and lost oxygen, causing more mental problems. Yet she has also defied medical science and survived through several illnesses and numerous operations.' He levelled Tommy with a serious look. 'Monica can't talk. She can't walk. She can't eat. She has to be fed through a special tube called a PEG tube.'

'With special food?' he asked.

'Exactly.'

'I've seen one of them before, I think.' He looked at Summer for confirmation and she nodded.

'Monica doesn't have a lot of normal things in her life but the one thing she loves best of all, the one thing that is guaranteed to make her happy, are clowns.'

'Clowns?' Summer and Tommy asked in unison.

'So every week the doctor on house-call duty comes out, not only to check how Monica is doing but to bring a bit of happiness into her life.'

'Laughter is the best medicine?'

'Yes. Monica is now in her twenties and since we've been performing what we like to call clown therapy,' he smiled as he spoke, 'she's continued to thrive as best as she can.'

'So where are the clowns? Are they inside the house?' Tommy asked.

'No.' Jason shook his head, his eyes alive with delight, and Summer felt a sinking in her stomach. 'They're inside this car.'

'You have clowns in your car?' Tommy was stunned.

'Ooh—too many answers to that question,' he murmured to Summer.

'*We* are the clowns, darling,' she pointed out. 'That's what Jason's trying to tell us.'

'We go inside. Get into the clown suits that are there, put on a bit of clown make-up and go and be clowns for Monica.'

'Ooh. I know a good joke,' Tommy said as they headed inside.

'Hit me.' Jason listened intently to the little boy but all the while was intent on watching how Summer accepted this task. She was such an elegant woman, with poise and grace. Would she dress up in a clown costume? He knew Amanda would have thought the whole idea ludicrous but, then, Amanda hadn't been a doctor so he never would have expected her to understand anyway.

Summer, however, was a doctor. Would she be able to accept laughter therapy as an alternative to general medicine? He hoped so. Tommy seemed enthusiastic and while Summer appeared highly reserved as she pulled her costume over her clothes, she didn't object.

They didn't have a costume for Tommy but Monica's parents managed to find some old clothes they adapted and even produced a funny hat with a flower sticking out of the middle.

'Hey, Mum. I'm just like Mr Calvin.'

Summer smiled. 'Yes, you are.'

'You totally have to take my photograph. I'm starting my collection *today*.'

'Ready?' Jason took Summer's gloved hand in his and looked into her eyes, which now had yellow diamonds painted around them. In the true classic clown style, she'd opted for a white base, a wide red grin and a soft red nose.

'I guess so, although I'm not quite sure what to do or say.'

Jason adjusted the Santa hat he wore on his head. 'Just let yourself go. Be happy. Remember, a smile can be contagious. So can laughter.' He gave her hand a little squeeze before they headed into Monica's room. She was half lying, half sitting on a specially designed bed, the sun coming in her window, the room painted brightly with pictures of clowns and balloons on the walls and ceiling.

'Hey, hey, hey,' Jason called, as he headed towards her. 'Is this the room of the magnificent Monica?'

Monica made a gurgling sound and slowly turned her head. Her face stretched into a bright smile and Summer's heart instantly filled with not only compassion but hope. It was amazing that the doctors of this community were willing to go to such lengths for their patients. This woman had nothing, needed everything, yet all she wanted was someone to make her smile… And she was now lying there smiling—because of Jason.

Tears were starting to gather in Summer's eyes and she knew that crying wasn't the order of the day. She pushed them aside and headed over to where both Jason and Tommy were doing their best to entertain Monica.

Tommy was dancing in a silly fashion around the room. Jason was trying to follow him but kept tripping over his large clown feet and every time he did, Monica would gurgle her approval. Summer joined in, feeling highly self-conscious at first, but after a few moments of seeing the delight radiating in Monica's eyes she threw caution to the wind and started telling jokes.

They laughed and joked around, sometimes falling over each other—slapstick would never die, she realised—and had the most fantastic time. When Monica's mother announced it was time for her midday nap, all three clowns were disappointed their routine was at an end.

'That. Was. Totally—'

'Buzzin'?' Summer and Jason finished together as they climbed into the car, waving a hearty farewell to Monica's parents.

'Yeah.'

After they'd changed out of their costumes and removed their make-up, Jason had shown Summer how to give Monica a check-up and what to specifically be aware of.

'How many more calls, Mum?' Tommy asked, completely animated.

Summer checked the list. 'Five left.'

'Aw. Is that all? Hey, can we go and visit Monica another day and be a clown again?'

Summer laughed. 'We'll see,' she replied non-committally. The atmosphere in the car was one of pure excitement as Jason drove them back towards town. The conversation was brighter, the laughter was deeper, and Summer couldn't help but look at Jason with admiration.

They worked their way through the remaining five house calls before heading back to their apartment. As they'd visited each patient, Jason had made notes on a pad which he now took inside.

'Come in for a coffee?' Summer suggested and he wasn't about to say no. He didn't want this day to end, the day when he'd realised that

Summer was indeed an extraordinary woman and one he appeared to be attracted to on multiple levels. It wasn't only her looks but her drive, her dedication and her delight in embracing her new life.

As she realised the time, she invited Jason to stay for dinner and soon he found himself standing alongside her in the kitchen, stir-frying. Cameron had never cooked, never shown the slightest interest in the activity, but, then, Cameron hadn't shown any inclination in spending time with his wife and son. As far as cooking went, it was something that had always helped Summer to relax and she could recall helping her mother prepare meals in their small kitchen at home. Of course, that had been before her father had made his fortune, a fortune forged through hard work as well as blood, sweat and tears. Cameron had inherited his wealth, as had his father before him. *That* had been the difference—inherited wealth versus earned wealth—and she knew she needed to find the right balance for Tommy. To give him a real inheritance, one built on friendships and trust.

She looked over at Jason, chopping vegetables

as he talked about his own family, recalling with humour about how his sister had once thrown a butter knife at him after he'd been teasing her. Could she trust him? Was he a man who valued honesty? Family? Monogamy?

From what he'd told her of his ex-wife, it was apparent he'd been badly burned in love once already. Had that made him bitter? Or, as she secretly hoped, had the ordeal made him stronger? Was he willing to explore this attraction that existed between them or was he simply stringing her along? She wasn't sure.

'How's the meat? Almost ready to do a dance with the vegetables?' he asked, his words bringing her back to the present.

'They are.'

'Smells fantastic.' He was close, her kitchen seeming to shrink as they stood close together, the aromas from the sizzling food filling the air. She could feel the warmth from his body and a deep-seated need flooded her within. What would it be like to kiss him? It wasn't the first time she'd asked herself that question and they'd certainly been close enough to have given it a go the other week but that was then…this was now. When his arm accidentally brushed hers, Summer gasped and placed her hand over the area as though burnt. She stepped away.

'Are you all right?'

'Sure. Uh…I'll go get my son off the phone.' She shook her head, forcing a smile. Tommy had asked to call Bradley the instant they'd arrived home and was still telling him about the totally buzzin' day he'd had. 'Not that I'm complaining, but since he's ventured out of his shell a little, my phone bill has increased.'

Jason chuckled at her remarks as she called to her son. 'Off the phone, please, and come and set the table.' A moment later Tommy bounded into the room, doing his clown dance as he gathered the place-mats and cutlery. Whatever tension had previously existed, it evaporated into the aroma.

As they sat down to eat, she realised that where she had thought it might be a bit uncomfortable, having Jason sitting at her table, eating the food they'd prepared together, it wasn't. It felt right and she wasn't sure whether the clown therapy had helped wipe away her own inhibitions or whether it was an indication that Jason really did fit into her new world.

After dessert of cold sweet dumplings, which somehow tasted just as amazing as when they'd been warm and freshly made, Tommy headed off to get ready for bed.

'I'd best be going, too,' Jason remarked as Summer closed the door on the dishwasher and turned it on.

'Because, of course, you have such a long way to go home.' Summer smiled at him and filled the kettle. 'Stay for a cuppa.' She didn't wait for his answer but took two cups down from the cupboard.

'I don't think I should.' He was finding it difficult to take his eyes from her as she moved comfortably around the kitchen which was the mirror image of his own.

'It's just a cup of tea, Jason.'

'I know.' Still, he was finding it difficult to move. She stopped and looked up at him, straightening as she withdrew the teapot from the cupboard and put it on the bench.

'What's wrong?'

'There's nothing wrong, Summer. It's been

an incredible day but…' He shoved his hands into his pockets, the way she'd seen him do so many times before, but this time she realised he only did it when she was close, as though he was trying to stop himself from touching her.

'Oh.' At the dawning realisation in her eyes, he nodded.

'Yes. Oh.' His gaze dropped to her lips, so luscious, so full, so close. It would only take a few steps to close the distance between them, to haul her into his arms and press his mouth to hers, the way he'd been wanting to do for quite some time now. He'd managed to stop himself in the past but after such an incredible day, and with the way she was staring at him as though that was the only thing she wanted him to do, he wasn't sure he'd be able to be the strong one this time.

'You are an amazing woman, Summer Hoyts.' At his words, she dipped her head and shook it slightly. 'No.' He stepped forward and lifted her chin so their eyes could meet. 'Don't brush my words aside. They're true. You were brilliant today. You related magnificently to all of the patients, you encouraged your son, you supported me. You listened, you applied and you dressed up as a clown to make a very ill woman smile.' His fingers stroked her cheek.

'Jason?' she whispered, and he could see the pain and confusion in her eyes.

He shook his head. 'What did that husband of yours do to you? How can you have no idea of how beautiful you are? Did he not appreciate you? Did he not want you?'

Summer knew he wasn't asking the questions to find the answers as he appeared more astonished to even *have* the questions in his mind in the first place. His eyes held a hint of wonderment mixed with confusion. She knew because it was exactly the way she felt.

'Whatever he said, you shouldn't believe him. Don't let anyone cut you down, Summer. That's the main thing I've learnt from my bad marriage. Believe in yourself. You *are* incredible.'

She'd heard words which had cut her down time and time again but she'd never received words that could build her up, as Jason's words were doing now. She was a person of worth and he was reiterating that. Her lips had parted at his intimate touch and her tongue slid out to wet her suddenly dry mouth.

'Oh, Summer, don't do that. You're difficult enough to resist as it is.'

Summer watched his mouth as he spoke, his words washing over her like a warm and comfortable blanket, making her feel both cherished and secure. Slowly, she raised her eyes until they met his. The desire was there. The need was there and Summer realised she didn't want him to walk away this time.

'Then don't,' she whispered, and slid her arms around his waist.

CHAPTER SIX

THE action was so out of the ordinary. So unlike her. Summer felt a wave of rebellious freedom wash over her. Never would she have ever dared to invite a man's attentions, even when she'd been married to Cameron. He had called the shots and after Tommy's birth those shots had vanished.

She closed her eyes for a second, not wanting to think about Cameron at all but wanting instead to focus on the man before her, the man who was helping her to come alive…in more ways than one. He not only supported her at work but the simple fact that he found her desirable—a desire she could see quite clearly in his rich, dark eyes—boosted her self-confidence as well as her self-worth.

Her fingers were lightly touching his back, their bodies were close, as close as they'd been the other week, but this time the conclusion seemed inevitable. They may have been fighting the attraction since they'd met but Summer had a blinding moment of clarity that whatever it was that existed between herself and Jason, it was imperative she discover exactly what it was. She was *meant* to do this. Add to the fact that she *wanted* to do this and it only made her *need* for Jason far more acute.

'Summer.' Her name was a caress on his lips as he traced the outline of her mouth with his thumb. She trembled and it produced a powerful protective reaction within him. He didn't want to hurt her. 'Are you sure?'

'Just kiss me, Jason. Please? Make me feel like a woman as only you seem to be able to do.'

That was a telling statement and one he promised himself he'd reflect on at a later time, but right now, when he had the woman who'd played a starring role in his dreams willing and pliant in his arms, he wasn't going to spend time worrying about anything else except doing exactly as she'd asked.

He brought his other hand up to cup her face and lowered his head to brush his mouth tantalisingly over hers. She trembled. She actually trembled at the touch and the effect was highly intoxicating, more so than anything he'd ever experienced before. Who was this woman and how did she seem to be able to tie him up in knots he had no hope of untying?

He tried it again, pressing his mouth to hers, accepting the sweetness she offered. The lightness of the touch was equally as powerful and although part of him wanted to rush ahead, to deepen the kiss, to hold her more firmly against his body while he plundered her mouth, another part of him wanted to savour this exquisite, tremulous moment.

She seemed to have invaded his thoughts and while they'd only known each other just over a month, it was as though they'd been designed for each other. The kiss would have only lasted the briefest of seconds but as time seemed to have stopped for the two of them, it felt like for ever. Half expecting him to want more, to take advantage of what was right in front of him, Summer was surprised when Jason seemed more than content to simply brush his lips lightly across hers again and again as though savouring the experience.

She wasn't immune to the charms of such an action, of the gentleness of his touch. In fact, it was more powerful than anything else she'd felt in her life. Soft. Feminine. Cherished. That was how his delicate touch made her feel and she couldn't help but shiver with anticipation.

'Jason.' She murmured his name against his lips and he accepted it, brushing on another kiss.

'Mmm.'

'Jason,' she whispered again as his hand slid around her neck towards her silky, soft hair. His feather-light kisses followed the path across her cheeks and down to nuzzle her neck. Summer's eyes were closed, her head had dipped back slightly and the feel of his fingers in her hair, the gentle massage at the base of her neck filled her body with a flood of tingles.

Her hands slid up his back as she brought her body into closer contact with his, her chest pressed against his, and he gasped, easing back slightly.

Summer instantly stilled. Had she done something wrong? She couldn't help it. It had felt right to want to have her body close to his but she was positive he'd moved away because she'd come closer. 'I'm sorry,' she murmured, and this time he drew back far enough so he could look down into her face.

'Sorry?' His voice was husky and filled with repressed emotion. 'What for?'

'Uh…' Her confusion increased. 'Because I…um…came closer.'

'Yeah. I know.' He nodded with approval.

She frowned a little more. 'But you moved away. I felt you.'

Jason could hear the uncertainty in her tone, could see mild fear in her eyes, and it was that which made him exercise even more self-control in order to ease his hold on her. 'What's wrong?'

'I don't want to…disappoint you.'

Now Jason was the one who was confused. 'Disappoint me? Summer, that's an impos-sibility. You are…dynamite, lady. Addictive dynamite at that.'

'Dynamite? Isn't that a bad thing?'

Jason laughed, the sound washing over her and offering up a smidgen of reassurance. 'What does dynamite do?'

'Explodes.'

'Exactly.' He looked at her for a moment and watched as dawning realisation crossed her face.

'Oh.' Her eyes were wide, her lips were parted, puckered into a little '*O*', and Jason couldn't help but press his mouth to hers once again.

'Mummy?' At the sound of Tommy's voice both Jason and Summer shifted quickly apart and looked over towards the doorway where her son stood in his pyjamas, ready for bed. 'What are you doing?'

'Er…um…Jason and I were just…ah…talking.'

'I thought that was called kissing.'

'Uh…yes. It is. Jason was just saying goodbye.'

Tommy thought about that for a moment, then nodded his head. 'Yep. I remember. Sometimes people kiss when they say goodbye.' He was still thinking, though. 'But my father never used to do that. Not for you. Not for me.' His words were matter-of-fact, without a hint of concern, but even that, as far as Jason was concerned was wrong. When a child spoke about his father, it should be with joy and happiness, not with apathy. 'He was too busy.'

It was the first time Tommy had mentioned his father and Summer wasn't at all sure how to react, especially given that she'd just been kissing Jason. Her mind was in a spin, her lips were still tingling and her heart was pounding wildly against her ribs. She cleared her throat. 'Yes. Your father was a busy man.' Summer wasn't sure what to say next so she simply asked, 'So, teeth all brushed? Ready for bed?'

'Yep. Ready for a story.'

'OK. I'll just walk Jason to the door and then I'll be in.'

Tommy nodded, indicating he'd heard her, but he didn't move. 'Actually, Mum…'

She tried not to smile at the way he spoke because it sounded so very grown-up. That was Tommy. Seven going on seventy. Or at least, that *had* been Tommy. Since their move from Sydney, he was starting to be much more of a seven-year-old and that was worth everything. 'Yes?'

'Could…um…?' He was nervous. Summer could tell. It was how he used to get whenever he'd wanted his father's attention. Usually, if he'd asked Cameron a question, it had been brushed aside with a wave of a hand and the child had been told to go and ask his mother. Then Tommy had stopped asking anything at all.

'What is it?' she encouraged.

'Can JD read me a story tonight?' The words came out in a rush and Tommy edged a little closer to Summer, as though needing her as a barrier or shield in case Jason refused.

'Oh?' Summer immediately looked at Jason and was not only surprised to note that she didn't feel at all self-conscious, given that they'd previously been caught kissing, but that the look which crossed his face was one of absolute delight at her son's request. 'Sure. If that's all right with Jason.'

Tommy turned to face him, taking in a deep breath to ask his earnest question, even though he had all but edged behind Summer in case he should be rejected. 'JD, would you mind—'

'Reading you a story?' Jason finished as he rushed forward to scoop the boy up into his arms and then sling him around so that Tommy now rode on his back. Both Summer and Tommy were taken by surprise at the sudden movement, but a split second later Tommy was laughing, his arms securely around Jason's neck.

'Say "Giddy-up" and we'll be on our way to a magical land created by our imaginations.'

'Giddy-up,' Tommy called, and Summer could only shake her head and smile. How was she supposed to get him to sleep when he was hyped up like this? Thank goodness it wasn't a school night.

Summer decided to give them a bit of privacy and took the opportunity to go and freshen up. When she looked at herself in the mirror, she was surprised to find her cheeks were still warm with colour and her eyes bright with excited anticipation. How could such a transformation have occurred by just a few amazingly tantalising kisses from a man she couldn't stop thinking about?

'Very easily,' she answered with a grin, although it slowly faded as her mind started ticking over with a thousand other questions. What happened now? Were they a couple? Dating? Would he want more? Was she capable of giving it? How would Tommy react if she did start dating Jason? How would they spend time together? Would anybody else know? Would anybody else be able to tell that she'd been kissed with such promise just by looking at her?

She closed her eyes and tipped her head back, not wanting to think about such things at the moment. Instead, she went and stood in the doorway to Tommy's room. It was so incredibly strange to see Jason in there. He was sitting up against the headboard on top of the covers while Tommy snuggled down beneath. He held the book open, pointing out different things in the pictures. It was a book about different fighter jets and where Summer often frustrated her son by not fully comprehending the absolute importance of not getting an F1-11 and an F15 mixed up, Jason appeared to understand everything with perfect clarity.

'It's the Rolls Royce of fighter jets,' Tommy was saying, and Jason agreed.

'I have always been partial to the old Spitfires.'

'Aw, they're awesome.'

'Totally buzzin',' Jason said with a smile. 'I went up in one once.'

'No way.'

'Way. A Spitfire. My dad arranged it with one of his buddies. I was a teenager and old enough to fly but it was…' He thought back and Summer watched as a far away look came into his eyes. 'It was like I was flying.'

Tommy laughed. 'Yeah, but you *were*.'

'No. I meant the feeling that absolutely nothing could go wrong. That all was right with life and the world. It was freedom and happiness all mixed into one with a large helping of adrenaline.'

'Have you ever felt like that again?'

Jason pondered that question for a moment and, without turning his head, he lifted his eyes and met Summer's and she realised he'd known she was there all along. 'Once—and quite recently, too. It was just as scary. Just as exhilarating. Just as confusing.'

She stared at him, trying to figure out if he meant what she thought he meant. Was he equating the kiss they'd just shared to the euphoria he'd felt at being up, no doubt looping the loop, in a Spitfire? Summer wasn't at all experienced in reading expressions, especially not where it pertained to her. She much preferred it if people just said what they thought, even if it brought pain. At least that way she knew exactly where she stood and could try to figure out a way to deal with things. Such as the time Cameron had brutally told her the truth about the origins of their marriage. Where she'd always thought he'd truly loved her, he'd blatantly told her otherwise. The truth had been hard to swallow but she'd pulled her life together and got on with it. That's what she seemed to have been doing for so long.

Now there was Jason, looking at her as though she were someone special. *Was* she someone special to him or did he want something else from her? It was clear there was an attraction between the two of them but attractions faded, people changed and hearts were broken.

No one moved. Jason stayed where he was and Summer found it impossible to get her mind to work at all. Tommy was oblivious to the two of them as he continued to study the pictures in the book. So much seemed to be being said but no words were spoken out loud. Jason's gaze dipped momentarily to her parted lips and the action caused a blush to wash over her from head to toe. When he looked at her like that, she was tempted to forget all about the sensible things of life and let herself go. She couldn't remember a man ever making her feel this way and *that* was surely something to think on further.

When Tommy yawned, it was enough to break the moment and both Jason and Summer moved at once. He stood from Tommy's bed as Summer bustled in.

'It's time to turn out the light,' she told her son. 'Say goodnight to Jason.'

'Why do you call him Jason, Mum? He told me he likes JD.'

'It's a nickname,' Jason told him. 'Just like your name is Thomas but everyone calls you Tommy.'

'Not everyone. Well, everyone here does,' he added. 'But back in Sydney I was always called Thomas. Mum's the only one who called me Tommy but now I like it all the time because we came here for a new start, didn't we, Mum?'

'We did, darling. Now…' she took the book from him '…say goodnight and I'll turn out the light.'

'Goodnight,' he murmured, smothering another yawn. Summer bent down and brushed a kiss across his forehead.

'Goodnight, Tommy. Dream you can fly,' Jason instructed.

'Sleep well.' Summer headed to the door and switched out the light, the room still being illuminated by a small nightlight plugged into the socket by the bed.

'Don't close the door,' he reminded her.

'I won't.' Summer and Jason headed into the lounge room.

'Is he afraid of the dark?'

'Not really, but most children his age like a nightlight.'

'Was his bedroom door closed at your place in Sydney?'

'Cameron would close it. He said that all people needed privacy.'

'Summer, I'm sorry if this is out of line but it doesn't sound as though your husband liked his son all that much.'

She shrugged and crossed to the lounge. 'He didn't. As far as Cameron was concerned, Tommy's whole purpose for being on this earth was to be heir to the family fortune. In having a son, Cameron had done his duty. That was it.'

'Carrying on the family name?'

'Exactly. It wasn't Cameron's fault that he was the way he was. It was how he'd been raised. He didn't know any different. To Cameron, money was the greatest commodity and with it all things were possible. That's exactly how it used to be with Cameron's father and grandfather as well.'

'Why do you defend him?'

Summer pondered the question, not answering right away. 'Habit, I guess. Needing to justify to myself why he is the way he is…or was.' She looked away.

'So Tommy is the heir to the Hoyts throne?'

Summer sighed a very heavy sigh. 'You could say that.'

'I'm surprised you were able to take him away from Sydney, then. What about Cameron's parents? Didn't they object?'

'They did. They objected so much they took me to court.'

'What?'

She shrugged. 'It's over with now. The judge gave me sole custody.'

'And rightly so.'

'He said that Tommy had been through enough trauma and until he was eighteen years old he would remain in my care. All the money is tied up in trust funds for Tommy and that's where it'll stay. I was offered all sorts of incentives but I wasn't going to take anything from Cameron's parents, especially after they tried to take my son from me.'

'Trauma?' Jason had stuck on the word, only half listening to everything else she'd said.

Summer looked down at her hands and was surprised to find them clenched tightly together.

'If it's too painful or I'm intruding too much, just tell me to back off.' Jason crossed to her side and sat next to her but made no effort to touch her. It was as though he needed to be close but not too close.

'I want to tell you, Jason.' Summer looked into his eyes and knew this was the right thing to do. She'd seen how Tommy had bonded with Jason, she'd seen how Jason had taken an interest in her son, and for that reason alone she wanted him to know why her son was the way he was. She owed it to Tommy to do everything she could to ensure he had a fantastic future but first a lot of healing needed to take place. Taking a deep breath, she slowly let it out then said softly, 'In a nutshell, Tommy saw Cameron die.'

'What?'

'He was five and a half and he saw it all. Cameron had taken him out to the family's riding ranch and only then because half of our staff were off with flu and I was at work.' She shook her head. 'I knew I should have stayed home or just taken Tommy to work with me.'

'Hindsight.'

Summer nodded her agreement. 'Cameron reluctantly agreed to take Tommy with him which wasn't as big a deal as he made out as Tommy went to the ranch twice a week for his riding lesson. All Cameron had to do was to arrange for Tommy to have an extra lesson with the instructor. Instead, he forgot Tommy was there and so Tommy simply followed wherever his father went. They were at the lunging yards where the foreman was breaking in a very feisty stallion. The horse was on the lunging rope, the foreman had everything under control but, of course, that wasn't good enough for Cameron's ego.'

She closed her eyes and shook her head. 'Cameron took over from the foreman. Tommy was leaning against the corral fence and could see everything quite clearly. Cameron…he lost control of the horse. The beast was still wild. He shouldn't have taken over. He should have left it to the foreman who was trained to deal with such an animal.'

As she spoke, Jason noted that there wasn't any panic or hysteria in her voice. The words were spoken matter-of-factly, as though she were simply telling him a story about something that had happened long, long ago.

'He was trampled. Tommy watched everything, from the accident to his father being taken away by ambulance. No one noticed him until about ten minutes after the ambulance had left. He was sitting on the ground, hugging his knees, his face buried in them, rocking slightly and whimpering.' A tear ran down Summer's cheek and Jason swallowed over the lump in his own throat before brushing it away with the backs of his fingers.

'Cameron died in the ambulance on the way to the hospital. I was notified by a police officer at the end of my shift. His parents insisted the stallion be put down. They sold the ranch.' She closed her eyes and shook her head. 'I was only told about everything when I returned from the hospital at the end of my shift. Tommy had been left with the housekeeper at the ranch who had then managed to get in contact with the cook who had been sent by the staffing agency to fill the void while everyone else was off sick. My son was transferred from one person to the next like a sack of flour.'

Jason found he was speechless but the need to protect this woman, to show her that not all people were so callous or unthinking, was over-whelming. He shifted and pulled her into his arms, holding her tightly against him, stroking her hair. She buried her face into his shoulder and for the first time in eighteen months the tears began to fall.

She hadn't realised just how much she'd needed to get it out of her system, to talk to someone about it, someone who wasn't a psy-chiatrist paid for by the Hoyts family. Jason had listened. Just listened, and she realised that it had been a long time since anyone had actually just listened to her. Now he was holding her, murmuring reassuring words. It wasn't sympathy. It wasn't empathy. It was just honest-to-goodness, old-fashioned caring, and Summer found it hard to remember the last time someone had held her like this, had cared like this. Cared about *her*.

'No wonder you needed to get out of Dodge.'

She smiled at his words and then found herself chuckling a little. 'You're not wrong.' He reached forward to the tissue box on the coffee-table and tenderly dabbed at her eyes, before giving her another one so she could blow her nose.

'I'm sorry. I didn't mean to cry all over you.'

'Hey. I'm sitting on a lounge with a beautiful woman in my arms, being a hero. Do you think I'm going to complain about you soaking my shirt?'

Her smile broadened at his words. 'How do you always seem to know exactly the right thing to say?'

'It's a gift,' he said with a wink and a smile. 'I've tried to bottle it, sell it, register it on the stock market, but it appears to be a gift only for me, and only to be taken out and used on very special occasions.'

She giggled. 'I'm glad this qualifies as one of them.' She withdrew another tissue and dabbed at her eyes. 'I must look a mess.'

'Quite the contrary.' He tenderly brushed her hair back from her face, tucking a stray strand behind her ear.

'How can you say that? I've just been blubbering all over you.'

'First I'd like to point out that that was hardly blubbering and, second, don't you get it by now? I think you look sexy no matter how you're dressed or how much make-up you're wearing.'

He thought she was sexy? 'Even if it's a big red clown face?'

'Even if it's a big red clown face,' he agreed.

'What do we do now?'

'I'm not sure. We like being with each other. Right?'

She was surprised, when she looked into his eyes, to find a hint of uncertainty. He'd told her that he and his ex-wife hadn't had the best of marriages and she was beginning to realise that when it came to affairs of the heart, he was as wary as she was. 'Right,' she confirmed, and received a sexy smile, mixed with a hint of relief, as a reward.

'Good. So, I'd like to suggest that we spend some time together. Talk. Really get to know each other. And Tommy, too,' he added quickly. 'I don't want you to think that I'm brushing him aside. I'm not. I think your son is quite amazing and definitely unique.'

'No argument from me. He's come along in leaps and bounds since we arrived and today, especially, was good for him.' She nodded as she mentally ran through their day. 'It was good for me, too.'

'You were amazing.'

'I think we covered this topic before.'

'And I seem to remember that I enjoyed the outcome of that conversation so I have no problem going over old ground.' He waggled his eyebrows up and down at her and she laughed again. 'I like the way you laugh.'

'I like the way you make me laugh.'

'Seems to me that you deserve it.'

'And what about you? Don't you deserve to find a little bit of laughter in your life?'

'Me? I've got tons. Regular clown I am.'

'Hmm. Tomorrow it's your turn.'

'Turn for what?'

'The post-mortem of your life. We'll get together—you can cook us dinner and then after Tommy's gone to bed, you can spill the beans about your life. In turn, I promise to comfort you, to stroke your hair and murmur soothing words.'

'Really?'

'Yes.'

'It's a deal.'

Summer stopped for a second, her eyes widening. 'So we're going to do this?'

'Rehash my bad marriage?'

'No. I mean this. Us.'

'We're going to get to know each other, yes. Take a step back into the ring of relationships, put our hearts out on the line and hope and pray they don't get trampled in the process.'

'I'll walk with a very light tread,' she promised.

'Dr Hoyts, I'm very pleased to hear that.'

CHAPTER SEVEN

WHEN Jason lay in bed that night, hands behind his head, staring up at the ceiling, he reflected on the events of the day. House calls were usually good fun, especially Monica's, but today, having Summer and Tommy along had made everything bright and vibrant. It was something Jason realised had been missing from his life since Amanda had walked out to pursue a life without him in it.

When they'd first started going out, Amanda had been happy with her life and they'd fallen in love quickly, marrying just as speedily. She'd seemed happy living in Ballarat, while going to Melbourne to do the occasional fashion show. For their first year of marriage everything had been perfect.

'Too perfect,' he muttered into the darkness. Amanda had wanted to wait a few years before they started their family to at least give her time to secure some regular modelling assignments. Then she'd been *discovered*. When she'd changed agents, it had been as though she'd changed lives. Her career had become her focus, not him, not the family they'd one day planned to have. It hadn't been until after their move to Melbourne, when he'd begun to see things as they really were, that he'd realised this wasn't the life he wanted to lead.

'Come with me,' she'd squealed happily after delivering the news that she'd been accepted for the European fashion show season.

'I can't, Amanda. I have a job. Patients.'

'Oh, tush. You can get a job anywhere in the world, Jason. We can base ourselves in Milan, you can work there and I can get to all the shows I need to.'

'And children? What about the family we've been planning to have?'

'*You've* been planning. Not me. Children would wreck my figure.' She'd brushed his words aside, then added, 'I suppose if you're that desperate to have a child, we could always adopt one, but it has to be a really cute one. Oh,

I know.' She'd clapped her hands excitedly. 'One of those children from China or Vietnam or something like that. It's all the rage. Oh, and a cute little moppet would look amazing in the photographs. We could do a big spread about how we've adopted a child and the media would love it.' She'd danced excitedly around the apartment, not caring that he'd been completely appalled at these suggestions.

Even now, years later, his stomach still churned at the memory. Children weren't commodities. They weren't purchased like handbags. They weren't merely born to provide an heir to the throne.

Jason thought about Tommy and what Summer had told him. No wonder she'd wanted to get the boy away from Sydney, from people who weren't interested in Tommy as a person but rather as a possession.

When he'd first met Summer, he'd thought she was like Amanda in many ways but the more he'd come to know her, the more he knew she had very little in common with his ex-wife. Summer was a mother first and foremost. She would do anything to protect her son—even if it

meant going up against the Hoyts family. She'd
done it and she'd won. That told him she wasn't
a push-over, that she was willing to stand up and
fight for what was important. It also told him she
had her priorities straight. Tommy came first.

He'd had so many questions when he'd first
met Summer and many of them had been
answered, but now there was one which kept
whirling around and around in his head. From
what she'd said about her marriage, it hadn't
sounded at all happy. So why had she stayed
with her husband?

The woman had intrigued him from the beginning and now that he'd kissed her… Jason
held his breath as he remembered the way she'd
trembled in his arms. So willing, so soft, so delicious. Her lips seemed to have been made to
fit his and even now, when he ran his tongue
over his lips, he could still taste her.

Was it possible that he'd stumbled across a
woman who was for real? Had she been faking
her reaction to him? Playing him like a fiddle?
He frowned, his gut instinct telling him she
wasn't like that at all. She'd been hurt in the past,
no doubt duped. Or at least that was the way *she*

told it. Jason had learned long ago that there were two sides to every story. As far as he was concerned, his marriage had come crumbling down because Amanda had changed. Not only who she had been but her ideals and plans for her future. She'd rejected him in favour of her career. As far as Amanda was concerned, Jason had been inflexible in his expectations of her, not willing to give up his career in favour of hers.

The next question he had where Summer was concerned was whether he could believe her. Believe what she'd said about her marriage? About her life in Sydney? Trusting a woman, and especially one he was obviously attracted to, was something he hadn't planned on doing again. He'd trusted Amanda and had had his heart broken. Could he trust Summer? Really trust her?

Time would tell.

As it turned out, Summer wasn't able to spend time with Jason on Sunday as he was called in to the hospital.

'Sasha sustained a fall and her parents say the cast's cracked,' he told Summer over the phone.

'Is she all right?'

'She's fine. Sally's the one who's upset.'

'Oh, the poor dears. Do you need me to come in?'

Jason thought about that for second. He wanted to see Summer, there was no doubt in his mind about that, but it was her day off and she deserved to have a rest. He needed to do X-rays and re-set Sasha's cast, and he knew it would be much easier with two doctors on board. He could always get his registrar up and out of bed but the poor man had only just finished the night shift.

'I'll come in. I'll get Tommy organised and be there soon,' she decided when he didn't instantly reply.

'Actually, yes. I think that will be best.'

'We can make sure she's completely still while re-setting the cast, if that's all that needs to be done.' Summer confirmed his own thoughts and again, it only served to emphasise just how in tune they seemed to be with each other.

After she'd rung off, she told Tommy they needed to go to the hospital. 'You can stay in the playroom and start doing some Christmas craft if you like.'

Tommy looked less than thrilled about having to go. Perhaps she should have told Jason she couldn't come in. In all honesty, they both knew he didn't specifically need her to be there. He could have grabbed Alyssa or Rhonda or one of the other nurses, orderlies or interns who were no doubt working this morning. They could have helped him as competently as Summer, but the truth was she wanted to see Jason.

She wanted to see how she would feel when she saw him. The fact that it would be at the hospital would be a good test. Before he'd left last night, they'd decided to get to know each other better, take things very slowly. They could call each other, arrange to spend time together, but Summer had asked him not to kiss her.

'You are kidding, right?' Jason had simply stared at her. Now that he'd finally given in and tasted her, how was he going to stop?

'No. You see, when you kiss me, I forget everything. I mean *everything*, Jason, and I'm not used to that.'

'Not used to kisses that curl your toes and turn your mind to mush?'

'No.'

Again, that told him so much about her marriage. What had she been? A trophy wife? She was certainly pretty enough, intelligent enough, accomplished enough—but she was also so much more than that. Had her husband been completely blind? Fool.

He'd brushed his thumb over her lips and then dropped his hand and backed away. 'Neither am I.'

'Well, that's good, then.'

'How is it good when you won't let me do it?' He smiled as he spoke and that was something else Summer needed to get used to. Never before had Cameron teased her, joked with her or spoken playfully about something like kissing.

'It won't be for ever. Just…for now.'

'The drought will be broken?'

'At some point. When we're both a bit more comfortable with this…thing between us.'

'You're making it sound like a disease.'

Summer had laughed. 'One we've both apparently caught.'

Jason had taken her hand in his and his eyes had been intense as he'd said softly, 'At least it's not one-sided.'

And that told her so much about his marriage. Had his wife thought it exciting to marry a doctor? Had it been a certain social status she'd been after? He'd obviously been in love with Amanda but the feelings hadn't been reciprocated in the same way. Did Amanda know what she'd lost? Fool.

'I'm ready,' Tommy said as he walked over to the door, waiting impatiently.

'Oh. Yes. Right.' Summer rushed around and grabbed her bag and her keys. She'd been so busy daydreaming about Jason that she'd forgotten what she was supposed to be doing. When she had everything, she stopped and looked at her son, her smile bright. 'Cheer up. I shouldn't be too long.'

Tommy was looking at her as though she'd grown an extra head.

'What?' She jangled her keys from her finger but didn't move.

'You're smiling more and more again.'

Summer nodded. 'So are you.'

'Not right now, though.'

'Oh, come on. You know you're going to have a good time making decorations. Jason said there are heaps of books and designs you can do. The other kids will be doing some, too, and already the ward is starting to look more and more Christmasy.'

Tommy eyed her carefully. 'And I'll get to see JD?'

'Sure.'

Tommy nodded and opened the door. 'OK, then. I'll go willingly.'

'Because you know you'll get to see Jason?'

'Yeah.' Tommy was already in the hallway. 'I really like him, Mum. He's fun. I've never met a grown-up man who was fun before.'

'Neither have I,' she said softly as she followed him out, closing the door behind her.

Even before they entered the ward a little later, they could hear loud crying. Summer looked at Tommy who immediately started to slow his steps.

'That doesn't sound like fun, Mum,' he murmured.

'Come on. You can hide in the playroom.' Summer ushered her son in and saw Jason coming out of room three.

'Hey, there, Tommy.' Jason greeted her son

warmly with a high-five before turning to Summer. 'We're just about to take Sasha down to Radiology but Sally can't bear to be parted from her.'

'Let her come.'

'That was just what I was thinking and with you here, we'll be able to accomplish it. Their mother is still beside herself with worry and with Sally's loud cries it doesn't make the situation any better.'

'And Sasha?'

'As calm as a lamb.'

'Pain transference?'

Jason looked at her in surprise. 'Is that possible?'

'I've read an article on it and it did focus on identical twins.'

'Something to consider.'

'The mind is a powerful organ.'

'It is. First of all, let's get Sasha organised.' Jason was about to head back into room three when he stopped and pointed to where Tommy was in the playroom. 'Do you want Tommy to go down to Rent-A-Grand?'

'I didn't have time to call and check if that was OK.'

'Mum only has three kids there this morning and one of them is Bradley.'

'Really?'

'His mum got called in to work so he came, too.'

'Well, if Bradley's there, you can bet Tommy will want to go down.'

'I'll call my mother and get it organised for you.' He walked to the nurses' station. 'Why don't you go and see if you can work some of your soothing magic on Sally?'

'My soothing magic?' she queried.

'Hey. It works when you're near me.'

A smile spread over her face at his words. 'That's such a nice thing to say. You're so sweet.'

'Thank you.' Jason picked up the phone and watched her go into the room. It was only a few moments later that Sally's cries started to subside and he knew that Summer had done it again. She was so natural, so real with children and he'd watched the way she seemed to charm them all, no matter how old they were.

She'd certainly charmed him as well, with her cool, calm elegance, her intense, incredible beauty and her singingly sensual body. To say she had him in a whirl was an understatement and he was relieved that they'd managed to figure out some new guidelines for their burgeoning relationship. The fact that he could tell her she affected him, the fact that she could tell him he was sweet. These were right steps in the right direction. He hoped.

Once everything was organised, they headed to Radiology, keeping Sally as close to Sasha as possible, only removing her from her sister's side when the X-rays were being taken.

'See? She's all right,' Summer said reassuringly as she held Sally comfortably in her arms. The four-year-old had her arms about Summer's neck, her head on Summer's shoulder. 'Your sister is very brave and I am very proud of both of you.'

'Can Sashy come home tonight?'

'That's what Dr JD and I are going to check, but if she can't, how about both of you have a sleepover here in the hospital and you can help make some special Christmas decorations for the ward?'

'Really?' Sally was immediately interested

and as Jason watched, he knew that there would be no problems with admitting the twins for the evening. 'I love sticking and cutting.'

'And Dr JD told me there's going to be *glitter*.'

Sally's face lit up like a Christmas tree and Summer couldn't help but laugh at the sight. The four-year-old shimmed down to the floor and started jumping up and down, clapping her hands. '*Glitter!* I *love* glitter.'

'And there's that magic,' Jason remarked as they stood side by side, reading the radiographs.

'It's hardly magic, Jason,' she contradicted, but couldn't believe how wonderful his words made her feel. Whenever she was with him, she felt such an overwhelming sense of self-worth, of importance. He made her feel that she was someone other people not only liked but looked to for support. She pointed to the X-ray. 'Looks as though it's only the cast that has broken so that's good news. Do we need to give her a sedative while we apply the new cast?'

'She'll need to be completely still so, yes, sedation is the best bet.'

'It would be better if Sally wasn't in the room.'

'Agreed. Any bright ideas for getting her out?'

'Get her to make a special Christmas card for Sasha—and use lots of glitter.'

Jason nodded. 'Excellent idea. See. This is why I like having you around.' He leaned a little closer and brushed the tips of his fingers against her hand. 'You're brilliant,' he said softly, his breath fanning her neck.

It was wonderful being allowed to be so close to him, to not have to worry about mixed signals or anything like that. It was wonderful and it was new and she was enjoying every minute of it. 'You're not so bad yourself,' she murmured, watching his eyes darken with desire. He had eyes she could have gazed into for hours. She shook her head to break the moment. Now wasn't the time.

They managed to get Sally to follow Summer's suggestion while Sasha's cast was being reapplied. When the little girl was back in the ward, still groggy from the sedative, Sally gave her the card—dripping with glitter—and was rewarded with a tired smile from her twin.

'That's them settled,' Jason remarked as they headed out to the nurses' station so he could write up the report.

'I guess it is.'

'Got any other plans for the day?'

'Well, I promised Sally I'd make some Christmas decorations with her, which might not be a bad idea while Sasha's sleeping.'

'And speaking of decorations, I noticed last night that you don't have any up in your apartment.'

'That's probably because I don't have any.'

'What? No decorations?'

'Do you have them up in your place?'

'I put them up in October. I love Christmas. I'd decorate the ward far earlier than the beginning of November if Rhonda would let me, but she won't and that's all there is to it.'

Summer smiled at him. 'You're like a little child.'

'Duh. Why do you think I work with them? That way, I have the most perfect excuse for never growing up.'

'Peter Pan?'

He grinned. 'Something like that. Why don't you go and get Sally while I do these notes and I'll meet you in the playroom.'

'I was going to ask Tommy and Bradley if they'd like to come and join in.'

'Good luck. They were playing games on the computer not long after I took Tommy down.'

'Hmm. Computer games versus making Christmas decorations.' She held out her hands as though they were scales and pretended to weigh the options.

'As I said, good luck.' Jason set about writing up the notes but lifted his head and watched Summer walk towards Sasha's room. He loved the way she moved. It was so lithe, so calm, with a ballerina's grace. He recalled her mentioning she'd done ballet as a child so that was obviously where she'd learned to carry herself that way.

Had she also done deportment? Gone to finishing school? Wasn't that what all good young ladies did? She'd told him quite a bit about her life with Cameron but he realised he didn't know anything about her childhood, about her parents. He knew she didn't have siblings but had obviously wanted some. Were her parents as equally as wealthy as the Hoyts family? He couldn't see the heir to the Hoyts fortune choosing a 'nobody' for his bride so Summer certainly had to have come from money somewhere down the line. He didn't even know her maiden name.

Of course, receiving the answers to these questions would no doubt only serve to increase the strong feelings he was beginning to have for her. Where he'd warned himself not to get involved, where he'd cautioned himself to learn from his past mistakes, not to go down the same road again—none of it seemed to matter when Summer was around him.

She most certainly wasn't what he'd first imagined. She had far more depth, more character, more compassion in her perfectly manicured little finger than Amanda had possessed and he'd do well not to continue comparing them, but the fact of the matter was that Amanda had been his wife, had been a woman he'd had incredibly strong feelings for, had thought himself completely in love with, and it had all turned out to be a farce.

Summer wasn't a farce. She was real. She was honest and in a lot of ways there was also a naiveté about her that appealed greatly to his male protective instinct. She was a good mother, wanting to help her son in any way she could, and Jason knew the seven-year-old boy was quickly becoming a favourite with him. There was such intelligence behind his blue eyes mixed with a lot of pain. Now that Summer had explained what had happened, what Tommy had witnessed, Jason understood that look and knew that if Tommy ever needed help, he'd be more than happy to provide it.

'You actually need to *move* the pen to get it to work, Jase.'

He turned and looked at his sister as she leaned over the top of the desk. 'Howdy.'

'Howdy back. You were lost in thought. Go anywhere nice?'

Jason's grin increased but he didn't say anything. 'What are you doing here?'

'Came over to see if the parents were free for lunch, but they're busy and mentioned you were in the ward so…here I am.'

'And you're just in time. We're doing more Christmas decorations today.' He pointed to the ones that had been made during the week, which were hanging from the ceiling. A few paper chains graced the walls but the ward needed more.

'Ooh, you *are* right. I *am* just in time.' Cassandra clapped her hands and rubbed them together. 'Come on, then.' She held out her hand to him. 'Let's go. Glue and glitter await.'

Summer came out of Sasha's room, holding Sally in her arms, and almost dropped her when she saw a strange woman reaching out for Jason. She watched as he smiled brightly, stood and took her hand in his. Who was this woman? What was going on here?

Her mind instantly jumped to three thousand different conclusions and all of them included Jason breaking her heart. Well, why not? Cameron had done it. Cameron had smiled sweetly at other women, had taken their hands, and when Summer had confronted him, had asked him to explain, he'd flatly denied any rumours about affairs and made her feel as small as lint for even daring to question him.

Surely she hadn't made another mistake? She didn't think she could handle it right now. No. Jason wasn't Cameron. Jason wasn't Cameron. She needed to say the words over and over to try to get her mind to at least settle down.

Sally put her hand on Summer's face and forced her head around. 'The playroom's over there, Dr Summer.'

'Of course it is.' Why did her legs feel so unstable? Why were Jason and the woman he was now openly holding hands with walking towards them?

'Summer. Come and meet my sister,' Jason called.

'Sister!' The word was out before she knew it and as she'd reached the playroom, she put Sally down. 'You get the paper and the scissors out again. I'll be there in a moment.' Sally ran off to do that.

'Hi. I'm Cassandra. Jason's little sister. You must be the new doctor from Sydney.'

'Summer. It's a pleasure to meet you.'

Jason let go of Cassandra's hand so she could shake Summer's but looked at his new colleague with a quizzical expression. He hadn't missed the look that had crossed her face when she'd seen him walking with Cass. What had it meant? Because from his experience in reading people, he'd seen that sort of expression before and in the past it had often been jealousy.

Summer? Jealous?

No. He had to have been wrong because if Summer was jealous then that would mean she had real feelings for him. Stronger than he or even she had realised. He shook his head and realised that both women had entered the playroom and were now chatting quite comfortably. Summer crossed to an internal phone on the wall and dialled a number, no doubt trying to convince Tommy and Bradley to come to the ward and join them for some craftwork.

'She's gorgeous,' Cassandra murmured quietly, taking in Jason's expression, the way he'd watched Summer move. 'She's the reason you've been so distracted lately.' It was a statement and as Jason turned sharply to look at his sister, she laughed. 'You are so transparent. I could read you like a book. She's nice, Jase.'

'You've just met her.'

'Then give me some time with her. Is she…someone I *should* get to know better?'

Jason's eyes were back to watching Summer. 'I don't know. Perhaps. Maybe.' When his sister gasped, he decided he needed a little room to breathe. 'I'll go get some of the other children who wanted to make decorations,' he said, and quickly left.

He headed to a few of the other wards to see

if there were any children visiting who might want to join in. After all, there were a lot of Christmas decorations to be made by the budding artists of Ballarat. The more, the merrier. When he returned, it was to find the playroom crowded, every chair taken, and even a few of the smaller children sitting on grown-ups' knees. Both Tommy and Bradley had indeed come up and he knew it was no doubt due to some fancy footwork and motherly ma-nipulation from Summer.

Summer herself had Sally leaning on her from one side and another little boy of about five on her other side. The boy had his arm about her neck and was intent on whispering a secret in her ear. By the smile, big and bright, on Summer's lips, he could tell she was enjoying every moment.

Paper chains had been cut, looped and then stuck together. Stars had been cut out. Candy canes, Christmas puddings, reindeer. The floor seemed to be covered with paper scraps and bits of glitter that had come unstuck from paper. Everything looked great but Summer looked amazing simply sitting there in the middle of the throng, listening intently to whatever great words of wisdom were being whispered in her ear.

'Dr JD. Dr JD.' He'd been spotted and headed over to help out where he was needed. He could feel Summer's eyes on him and he glanced over in her direction to find her smiling brightly at him.

'There you are. I was wondering if you'd been waylaid by an emergency.'

'No.' He knelt down on the floor, no doubt having now covered his legs with glitter, and started to fold a piece of paper. He kept folding until it was the right size and then picked up a pair of scissors, snipping expertly here and there. When he'd finished, he carefully unfolded it and received a round of applause when he held up a string of paper Santas.

'You have to teach me how to do that,' Tommy declared, coming to sit beside Jason. 'That's totally buzzin'. Right, Brad?'

'Totally,' Brad agreed, and both boys started folding paper and asking Jason for instructions.

Everything was perfect, Summer thought as she looked around. Cassandra was busy teaching some of the older girls how to layer paper at different angles to make different effects.

After talking a few minutes with Cassandra, she'd discovered she was a dressmaker in Melbourne but often came home for weekends, especially around Christmas. For a woman she'd just met, Cassandra had been very open and honest about her life and Summer idly wondered whether Jason had already told his sister about the latest developments in his life—namely his attraction to her. Either way, it was nice to be instantly accepted by someone who Jason obviously held in such high esteem and again Summer felt as though things were really starting to come together, starting to take shape—*her* shape.

She looked at Jason, who was teaching Tommy how to cut out paper Santas, and her heart swelled with love. Her son was so happy, so relaxed and she knew a lot of it was to do with the easy acceptance given by Jason. Jason, who had not only accepted Tommy but had accepted herself as well.

Easy acceptance. Brother and sister seemed to be cut from the same cloth. The people here, those she worked with, liked her for who she was—not for her family name. She was simply

Summer and it had been far too long since she'd felt that way.

Jason had figured it out, though. He knew of the Hoyts family, knew of their influence, and yet it hadn't fazed him one bit. He was caring and sincere. Helpful and honest. It was no wonder she was falling in love with him. It also helped that he was drop-dead sexy. She smiled to herself, acknowledging the extent of her feelings for him. For some reason, it didn't bother her. She was falling in love and although it was terrifying, it was addictively exhilarating at the same time. And it made her feel…truly alive.

CHAPTER EIGHT

FOR the next week, it was all systems go as far as Christmas fever went. Wards were strung with tinsel. Fake mistletoe was hung over doorways. Where some of the staff had previously been wearing Santa hats, they now seemed to be part of the uniform, and Summer loved every moment of it.

She'd learned how to make paper chains, how to cut out and make three-dimensional stars. Jason had given her and Tommy a lesson in how to not only cut out paper Santas but also baubles and bells, strings of them lining the wards. The fact that the children had made the decorations that were strung up everywhere in the paediatric unit only served to make the atmosphere more personally brilliant and festive.

Tommy's class at school were starting to wind down, getting ready for the approaching

Christmas holidays, which would see him enjoying seven weeks off. Again, she found it difficult to believe they'd only been in Ballarat for such a short time as it had been the happiest time they'd ever had.

Jason had been as attentive as ever and was now making plans to come over and decorate her house that evening.

'We both finish around five o'clock so I vote that we collect Tommy and then head to the shops to get you some decorations.'

'Brave the shops? At Christmas time? After work?'

Jason chuckled. 'This isn't Sydney, Summer,' he reminded her. 'Don't tell me, you used to do most of your shopping on line?'

'Well…yes. It was just easier.'

'Undoubtedly.' Jason winked at her as he twirled a pen in his hand. They were sitting in the ward, having just finished their afternoon ward round a little early as they didn't have that many patients in at the moment.

'It was,' she added, feeling compelled to defend herself. 'I had a full schedule in Sydney between work and charity events and it was difficult to get to the stores. Then there was Tommy and the house to keep organised, meals to be discussed with the cook, dress fittings to attend and—'

Jason held up his hands in a '*T*'. 'Whoa, lady. Time out. I was just teasing.' He took her hand in his as they were presently alone at the nurses' station. As soon as he touched her, Summer's mind emptied of all coherent thought as the warmth from his hand ignited a mass of tingles that travelled up her arms and exploded throughout her body.

It was getting worse. Her reaction to him was so immediate, so intense and so incredible...and she knew why. Ever since they'd met, she'd found herself dreaming about him, fantasising about him, and ever since he'd brushed those tantalising kisses across her lips, she'd found herself falling...falling head over heels in love with him.

As per her initial request, Jason had showed incredible restraint and hadn't kissed her again, although she could easily tell he wanted to just by looking at him. The fact that he'd abstained had shown her he had the willpower to do so. Add to that the fact that he still wanted to be with her and it had only caused her to fall for him even faster than she'd imagined.

Here was a man who listened to her. Here was a man who enjoyed being with her, spending time with her. Here was a man who clearly had a lot of time for her son, who was willing to read books with him, play games with him and, most importantly, listen to him. To say that Tommy thought the world of Jason was an understatement and ever since the day Jason had taken them out on house calls, Tommy had opened his locked-away heart and allowed someone else in.

Now she was having to tell her son off for normal boisterous behaviour, getting him to clean up his room.

'Summer? Earth to Summer?' Jason had a teasing smile on his lips as he waved his other hand in front of her eyes. When she looked at him, his smile increased. 'Where did you go?' He leaned closer. 'And can I come, too? You had such a dreamy expression on your face. Tell me you were thinking about me.'

Summer smiled shyly but didn't look away. This was Jason, not Cameron. This was the man who was really interested in her, cared about her. 'I was…thinking about you.' She sighed slowly. 'I seem to spend a lot of my time thinking about you,' she confessed. 'And when you touch me…' She looked down at their hands, her voice dropping to an intimate whisper. 'Even a simple touch like this…' Her eyes met his again and he was amazed at how intense her blue depths were.

'Summer. Don't say things like that.' He didn't move away. Instead, he brought his chair closer, his fingers entwining with hers in a promise.

'But it's how I feel. I can't help it, Jason. It's how you make me feel and I've never—*ever*—felt this way about anyone before. I don't know what I'm supposed to do. I don't know what the protocols are. You're my closest friend here and I can't help but tell you how I feel.'

'Summer, I meant don't say things like that when you've asked me not to kiss you. The way you're looking at me right now is fuelling a blaze deep down inside me—one that is threatening to rage for a long time once it's let out. My self-control is so taut that it's becoming a real test of my willpower just to work alongside you every day. The fact that I can touch you like this…' He squeezed her hand again. 'That I can be near you so your perfume drives me wild to the point of distraction does help, but at the same time it's adding more heat to the furnace.'

'Oh, Jason.' Summer swallowed at his explanation, her throat having gone dry due to her increased heart rate. How could words, words such as the ones he'd just spoken, create such havoc within her? 'I want you to kiss me,' she whispered, but still kept her distance. 'I really do and I think about it all the time.' Her eyes dropped to his parted lips as she spoke and she watched as his Adam's apple moved up and down his strong throat as he swallowed. 'But at the same time I need space.'

'I know. I didn't say that I didn't understand. I said it's getting more and more difficult.'

'You'll come over tonight? Hang the decorations?' Her words were still asked with a breathlessness she was desperately fighting to control.

'Yes.'

'And then we'll…talk again? Figure out what happens next?'

'Yes.'

'Together?'

Unable to resist her any longer, Jason lifted her hand to his lips and pressed a long kiss to it. He lifted his eyes to meet hers, her hand still warm from his breath which fanned over it. 'Together,' he confirmed. 'Whatever is happening between us, Summer, is definitely happening to both of us. That's the important part to remember. Neither of us is in this alone and so long as we're determined to take this ride side by side, we should be fine.' At least, that was what he sincerely hoped for.

'Not get hurt?' She desperately needed reassurance. Jason could see that. Sometimes when he looked into her eyes he was almost positive he saw love for him shining brightly and at other times he saw only fear. That was something else he needed to know. Just *how* had her husband hurt her? Had it been a matter of neglect or something more? Either way, he was beginning to realise that the pain and anguish he'd experienced with the break-up of his own marriage was completely different to what Summer had been through.

'Yes. Not get hurt,' he confirmed, and kissed

her hand again before reluctantly letting it go. The phone on the desk rang and he snatched it up quickly, needing a diversion for his thoughts. To say the woman beside him was special was becoming an understatement. 'Jason,' he said into the phone.

'Jason, it's Mags.' the triage sister said. 'We may have a problem here in A and E. Can you or Summer come down?'

Jason looked at Summer and mouthed, 'A and E,' so she knew who was on the phone. 'How about both of us?'

Mags chuckled. 'Can't bear to be parted, eh?' Jason held the phone closer to his ear, trying to ensure Summer hadn't heard. He knew she didn't want their attraction to be common knowledge around the hospital—not just yet at any rate—but she also hadn't realised that most of the staff were already aware that something was going on between the two paediatricians.

'We'll be there soon.'

The two of them headed to A and E. 'Did she say what was wrong?' Summer asked, glad to be doing something so she wasn't just sitting there staring into Jason's eyes.

'No.' He held open the door which led to the stairwell and together they descended towards the A and E department. When they arrived at the triage station, Mags was on the phone again and Jason leaned over her shoulder to see what she was writing down. 'Food poisoning?' He looked at Summer, who grimaced.

Mags finished her call, then turned to face them. 'All right. Here's the scoop. We're expecting quite a few students in from Eureka Heights High School with suspected food poisoning.'

'Symptoms?' Jason took the notes Mags had written down and scanned the details.

'Nausea, colicky abdominal pain. Two students have vomited.'

'Do we know what they've eaten?'

'Not as yet. All we know is that all the children who are sick ate from the school cafeteria at lunchtime.'

'Any other schools affected?' Summer asked.

'Not that I've heard. Ambulances are on their way with the worst cases. A few students have already been sent home.'

'I want to see everyone,' Jason stated. 'Those children who were sent home, find out who they are and get them in here for observation. If we can isolate the cause, it will go a long way.' He turned to Summer. 'When they get here, we need to monitor them for any other symptoms to make sure we're not dealing with anything more than general gastrointestinal tract contamination by a microorganism.'

'Botulism?'

Jason nodded. 'Watch for headaches, dizziness and especially lack of muscular coordination. You know the drill.'

'I do. We had a case of *Clostridium botulinum* in Sydney two years ago and three people died.'

Jason winked briefly at her. 'Then you're our experienced gal. Mags, if any of the staff have questions about patients or are overly concerned, Summer's the first point of contact.'

'Noted.'

The ambulance sirens could be heard as other nursing and medical staff went out to greet them. 'Let's get this sorted,' Jason stated, and they went to work.

They saw several students and after Summer had examined two, she was thankful no major symptoms of botulism had been reported.

'We still need to try to isolate the cause,' Jason remarked when they met up at the nurses' station, both of them writing up notes.

'I've just sent the contents of my patient's stomach to the lab for immediate analysis,' Summer told him.

'Ah…you are brilliant, Dr Hoyts.' He patted her hand and thankfully, for both of them, he didn't linger.

'Thank you.'

'Just got another call,' Mags put down the phone and turned to face them. 'Another school has reported students with similar symptoms.'

Jason looked to Summer. 'Perhaps it's not food related?'

She thought for a moment. 'This isn't necessarily bad information. Well, it's bad that more students are sick but it might help us to narrow down whatever is causing it. What do the two schools have in common? Are they close in location? Do they use the same water supply? Do they have a supplier of food in common? Do the students know each other in some way? Were they all at the local swimming pool last night?'

'You're right. We need to think bigger and differently. OK, Mags, can you get all staff gathered for a quick briefing, please?' Jason asked, and when everyone who was free managed to come together, Jason handed over to Summer. He was proud of the way she dealt with the situation, her tone commanding, her leadership strong. She wasn't overpowering or domineering, assuring everyone that she was available to review patients if they had any queries.

As he watched her, noticing the way she looked people directly in the eye when she spoke to them, seeing how she smiled at people, related to them so naturally, he couldn't help but be jealous.

It was ridiculous as she certainly wasn't flirting with anyone, but he was jealous of anyone who stole her attention from him. He liked it best when it was just the two of them, sitting, chatting and being. He was jealous of everyone who was with her when he wasn't.

It was a revelation and one he wished he could have had at a more opportune time, but as staff members began to disperse and more ambulances began to arrive, Jason could only sit there and look at her—look at the woman he realised he'd fallen in love with.

Impossible. He shook his head.

Incomprehensible. He forced himself to look away.

Inevitable. He immediately looked back, smiling when their eyes met.

'You handled that beautifully,' he reassured her, and watched as the lines around her eyes relaxed a little. 'You're a natural at public speaking.'

She rolled her eyes but smiled. 'I've had plenty of practice.'

'I guess you have. I feel as though there's a whole world of yours that I know nothing about.'

'And yet this world that I'm living in now is the only world where I feel truly happy.'

'You are?'

'Happy? Yes.'

'Happy happy?'

Her smile increased. 'Yes. You sound surprised.'

'Actually, I'm relieved more than surprised.'

'Why?'

It was his turn to smile. 'I'll tell you later tonight.'

'After we've hung the decorations?'

'Of course. Nothing can interfere with that.'

The phone on the desk shrilled to life yet again

and he quickly picked it up, his eyes still intent on Summer's. 'A and E,' he said. 'This is Dr Daniels.' He frowned, looked away from the tempting woman beside him, and picked up a pen, quickly taking notes. 'Yes, that's right. You've heard correctly. Two other schools have been affected.' He paused, listening. 'No, we're not sure what's going on as yet but if you'll bring the children in, that will help. Yes, all children who are complaining of abdominal pain and nausea.' He took a few more notes and then hung up.

'Ladies and gentlemen,' he said to the room in general. 'We have an epidemic.' He took Summer's hand in his and said softly, 'And the latest school affected is Tommy's.'

Summer's eyes widened for a moment before she nodded. 'Here's hoping he ate the lunch I packed for him this morning and not one from the cafeteria.'

'With your amazing cooking, I'm sure he did.'

Summer scoffed. 'Peanut butter and jam sandwiches are hardly classified as amazing cooking, Jason, but thank you.' She cupped his cheek for an instant to say thank you but then seemed to realise what she was doing and quickly dropped her hand back to her side.

Jason tried not to focus on her sweet touch, which took extra strength. He turned away from her. 'Where's the clerk?' Jason located the woman and gave her further instructions. 'Alert the health department. We're going to need the police here and at the schools. A hotline needs to be set up for parents who are concerned about their children or wanting to know what's going on. We'll need to get information out to all other schools, both private and public, not to serve food from their cafeterias. Get extra staff on this if you need to. Mags?' Jason turned around, looking for the triage sister. 'Mags. There you are. We've just had a call from another school. I'll need blood samples from everyone. We'll need to rule out contamination such as mercury or anything like that, which may have been in the water or food.'

He continued to talk to the sister and although Summer could quite easily stand there and watch the way he moved, his shoulders broad and straight, his hair just starting to curl at the edge of his shirt collar, his fresh spicy scent overpowering her senses, she knew she had to break away and concentrate on her job. There were patients to be seen. A mystery to be solved and lives to be saved.

They worked on, having so many students coming in to A and E that all staff were not only run off their feet but were starting to put some patients in the corridors as they simply didn't have the space in the treatment rooms.

Once test results started coming back from the now overworked pathology lab, stating that the culprit was a micro-organism detected in margarine used in all affected schools, they started sending the milder cases home, though Jason admitted two fifteen-year-old girls for further observation overnight who'd been among the first to report the symptoms.

'We've run out of the electrolyte icy-poles,' Mags reported. 'Neither do we have any more powdered sachets left. I've sent down to the supply stores for more but it's just frustrating.'

Summer nodded in understanding.

'Oh, how's your son?' Mags continued. 'He's not been affected?'

'No, thank goodness. I've checked with the

school and he should be either on the bus heading to Rent-A-Grand or already there.'

'Good to know.'

'In fact,' Jason said from behind her, 'my mother has just sent up a list of those children she now has in her care, in case parents call here wondering where their child is.'

'Excellent.' Mags took the list from Jason.

'Listen, Summer, we're settled here for the moment,' Jason said quietly. 'Why don't you go down and check on Tommy? Make sure he's really OK.'

'Really? Because that would be great.'

'Yeah. Go. I know you need to check on him.'

'Thanks, Jason. I'll just quickly finish these case notes so I don't forget then go straight down.'

As she spoke, he could see the gratitude in her eyes and he also thought he saw a hint of relief. Did she think he didn't comprehend exactly what Tommy meant to her? After she'd told him about her husband's death and how Tommy had been affected by it, it was clear to him that simply hearing that her son was all right wasn't enough. He not only appreciated her devotion to her son, he applauded it.

From everything he'd seen, she was a brilliant mother. Where Amanda hadn't liked or wanted children, Summer was the opposite. Tommy had been the one bright spark in an unhappy marriage and in a very small way Jason envied her that, wishing for one brief moment that he, too, could have been a father. Children were so important to him, so necessary to his life. He not only loved helping them at work, helping them to heal both physically and emotionally, but he loved talking to them. They were amazing, especially their insights into the world, and he'd found young Tommy to be both highly intelligent and a lot of fun to be around.

He had an urge to check on the boy himself but didn't want Summer to think he was intruding. Would she mind if he tagged along? Would he be overstepping the bonds of the friendship they'd forged?

Summer put her pen down and shut the case notes. 'There. Now I don't have to worry about them at least.' She stood and straightened her top. 'Still all quiet?'

'Sure is.' Jason smiled but crossed his arms

over his chest. 'Get going. I can't guarantee it's going to stay this quiet, so now is the time.'

'Yes. OK. Won't be long.' She turned and took three steps away then stopped and turned back. Aware that Mags and other staff members were about, Summer inclined her head. 'Want to come, too? If you've got time,' she quickly added. 'I don't mean to take you away from a patient. I just thought that…you might like to…check on Tommy, too, or some of the other kids.' She was talking too fast, something she rarely did, having been meticulously schooled in the art of conversation, but with the way Jason was looking her, as though he wanted to wrap his arms about her, pick her up and spin her around, the conscious effort to control the speed of her speech flew away with the fairies. 'Or not,' she added when he didn't say anything, and turned away again.

Before she'd taken one step, Jason was by her side. 'Thought you'd never ask,' he murmured as they headed out of the department. The easiest and most direct route was to go down the corridor towards the lifts. Neither of them spoke. The awareness between them seemed to be enveloped in a bubble that separated them from everyone else in the hospital, and when they entered the empty lift car, it only intensified.

As they stood there, side by side, Jason shifted and brushed his hand against hers. Summer sucked in a breath, all her nerve endings completely alert. It was just the way it was when Jason touched her, whether on purpose or accidentally. The main problem was, she was *wanting* to feel those tingles, experience those goosebumps, and she was still astonished at how, by a simple touch, he could reduce her to a mass of warm fudge... and she *liked* warm fudge.

Jason was overjoyed when she took his hand, brushing her fingers inside his, the awareness alive and alert between them. He looked at her lips, lips which were parted as though they were ready and waiting for him.

'Summer.' He shifted closer, his warmth enveloping her, cocooning her from everything else, protecting her. The background murmur of the lift as it moved slowly between floors was nothing compared to the pounding of his heart as he bent his head towards her.

He needed to kiss her. Couldn't she sense

that? He'd worked hard at earning her trust, of keeping his distance, of doing as she asked, but how could a man possibly resist such an elegant, ripe flower who appeared to be waiting just as impatiently for his caress?

'Summer?' This time her name was a question on his lips and after looking intently into his eyes, she realised the truth. Jason needed her to make the first move. He wanted her, needed her even—of that there was no denying—but he wasn't going to break her trust and at that moment Summer knew she could do this.

She could really put her heart out there again, knowing Jason wouldn't hurt her. *Trusting* Jason not to hurt her, just as he was trusting her not to hurt him. Love was nothing without trust and she knew that was where her marriage to Cameron had failed dramatically. Even though she'd thought she'd loved him in the beginning, there had been no trust.

That was not the case here and not giving herself the opportunity to psychoanalyse herself any further, Summer placed one hand on the back of his neck and impatiently brought his mouth down to meet hers.

CHAPTER NINE

THE instant they touched, Summer had the over-whelming sense that she'd finally come home.

She couldn't describe it, didn't understand it and wasn't going to fight it. His lips were warm and tender on her own. Soft and gentle, not that she would have blamed him if he'd taken her with a hot and hungry passion given the way they'd both been holding back from this moment, but like a man who had been crawling through the desert, dying of thirst, he obviously intended to sip thoroughly rather than guzzle greedily.

Every sense in her body seemed to be alive to the slightest pressure, the slightest touch, not only from his mouth but from his hands. He'd let go of her hand to rest his on her hips, the warmth of his palms radiating through her navy cotton skirt. He didn't want her to move, didn't want her to go anywhere except where she currently was. Here. Beside him. Letting him taste her sweetness.

And, oh, how sweet she tasted! The pleasures of Summer's mouth were infinitely more incredible than his memory recalled or his dreams had imagined. A mixture of flavours hit his senses as he continued to hold himself under control, wanting to burn every second of this long-awaited encounter into the far recesses of his mind.

She was close and warm and eager as he slowly coaxed her lips to open just a little more. His tongue touched the edge of her mouth and she shuddered in appreciation, her fingers at his neck ensuring he wasn't about to lift his head any time soon. It made him realise just how special she was and the fact that she wanted him, was willing to let him kiss her, spoke volumes for commitment to the emotions surging between them.

His thumbs at her waist started moving in little circles, creating even more heat which flooded her senses. As she managed to suck in some air, his scent increased her already over-active receptors and, sighing, she leaned closer to him, opening her mouth even more, the hunger she'd denied herself for such a very long time coming to the fore and urging her on.

Jason was pleasantly surprised when she leaned into him, letting him know she wanted more. Happy to oblige, he slid his arms around her back, bringing her body into even closer contact with his own. Both of her hands were in his hair as heat surged between them, their mouths becoming hotter and hungrier with each passing second.

As the lift continued to descend, both of them continued to soar. When they were together like this, life seemed to have a habit of standing still, as though only the two of them existed in the world, that what they felt when they were as close as they were now was all that mattered.

The faint 'ding' of the lift, indicating their ride was over, slowly penetrated Jason's hazy mind. Not wanting to be caught kissing his colleague— more for her sake than his own—he eased away from her. Both of them were breathing heavily and parted as the lift doors opened. Thankfully, no one was waiting and the corridor they exited into was clear. Jason took her hand and stopped her.

'Wait a moment. I just need to get myself under control before I walk into a room where both my parents are.' He ran his free hand through his hair, mussing it up so it was now sticking up at an odd angle. Summer smiled, her eyes still burning with heat for him. 'What?'

'You look…really sexy.'

'Summer,' he warned.

'I can't help it. I like the way you look. I'm heavily attracted to the way you look and when your hair sticks up like that…well, you make it difficult for a girl to resist you.'

'I don't want you to resist me, honey.' His cheeky grin only added to his appeal. 'I just want you to pause for a while.'

Summer laughed, enjoying the light-hearted banter. It was something she knew she'd have to get used to, or at least that she *hoped* she'd be able to get used to, as she spent more time with Jason. 'You make me laugh, Jason.' She reached up and pressed one last kiss to his lips.

'Don't start,' he warned, his breath catching in his throat at her quick action. 'We need to check on Tommy.'

'Yes. Yes. Of course.' She was a mother first and

foremost. She knew that. He knew that, but at the moment she felt more like a schoolgirl with her first crush and it was utterly exhilarating.

She felt like skipping down the corridor. Jason had kissed her—*really* kissed her—and it had been everything and so much more than she'd dared to dream about. Walking beside her was a man who honestly cared about her. It was definitely a change from how her life had been with Cameron and it was liberating.

When she entered Rent-A-Grand, Tommy came running over to her, embracing her instantly. Again, that was something he hadn't done since he'd been very small and as she looked down into his face, she noticed he had been rather scared.

'I'm OK, Mum. The teacher said it was only kids who'd eaten at the cafeteria and I didn't.' His words were brave but there was still a quiver in his tone.

'No. You didn't,' she reiterated. 'You're a good boy, my darling.'

'Brad had his own food, too, but Damian and Mike didn't. Are they OK? Are they still really sick? Mike looked green.'

Summer mentally recalled the two boys who had joined Bradley in Tommy's list of friends. 'They're both doing fine. I saw them both, spoke to their parents, and they'll be able to go home in about an hour's time. I just want to keep a watch on them for a bit longer.'

Tommy instantly relaxed at this news and turned to face Jason, who'd just finished having a word with his mother.

'Hey, there, champ.' Jason held up his hand for a high-five and then the two of them did some secret handshake thing which she'd caught Tommy practising the night before. 'Good. You remembered.'

'Yep. I taught Brad and I'm gonna teach Mike and Damian when they're better.'

'Good thinking.' Jason ruffled Tommy's hair. 'You feeling OK?'

'I'm fine.'

Still, as though he needed to be certain, Jason squatted down and pressed a hand to Tommy's forehead and got him to stick out his tongue. 'No tummy pains?' he asked.

'Nope.' Tommy shook his head for emphasis and Summer couldn't help but smile. Her boy was so much more relaxed, more at ease within himself. It was good to see and with the way he was relating to Jason…it made her heart turn over with love.

'Good to hear. How about coming back to my place for dinner tonight when your mum and I have finished working?'

'Can we have fish fingers?'

'Uh…' Jason looked up at Summer, who merely rolled her eyes. 'Sure. If that's what you'd like.'

'And when we go on our camping trip, we can cook them over the fire?' The up-and-coming camping trip had also been a big topic of discussion between the two of them, even though there was no firm date set.

'I'll teach you.'

Tommy put his arms around Jason's neck in a voluntary gesture of thanks, which had Jason looking instantly up at Summer as he held the boy close. Summer saw that Jason was overcome with emotion but held himself together at the unexpected embrace.

'Thanks, JD. You're the best.'

It was all over as quickly as it had begun as

Tommy ran off to tell Bradley the news about their friends. Jason stood, blinked twice and then looked at Summer.

'He has a way about him,' she remarked.

'He does.'

'He's going to do good things. I just know it.'

'Brains, charm and the Hoyts family fortune to inherit? I'll say.'

'And honesty. My son is a stickler for honesty.'

'A highly commendable attribute for a boy with big shoes to fill.' They both watched him for a moment, laughing with Bradley before they settled down to play a game.

Summer couldn't have been prouder of Tommy and it was moments like that which helped her to realise that removing him from the stuffy grammar school he'd been attending in Sydney had probably been the best thing she'd ever done. If he was going to be a great man, he needed to start on the bottom rung of the ladder by becoming a great friend, which was exactly what he was doing.

He was definitely a firecracker with an extremely sharp mind. Often he would speak not only with a vocabulary far exceeding his years but he appeared to have knowledge to match. At other times he seemed small and lost but Jason had complete confidence in Summer. He'd seen at first hand what a wonderful mother she was and the only thing he felt the boy needed was a strong, male role model. The big question was, how could he apply for the job?

When Tommy had hugged him, Jason's heart had leapt into his throat. Of course he'd been hugged in appreciation by his patients time and time again over the years, but there was something about Tommy that simply made everything far more personal. The fact that Jason was certain he was in love with Summer only made things more delicate. He'd made many mistakes in his life and he'd learned long and hard lessons from most of them, but he knew if he wanted to have these two people in his future, he couldn't afford *any* mistakes. They were just far too important to him.

The trip back to A and E was made in a companionable silence, both of them lost in thought. Without a word both of them avoided the lift and decided to take the stairs. Jason was acutely aware of Summer's presence beside him.

A new string of patients greeted them on their arrival and it was close to six o'clock before things started to settle down to a more normal level. In total, six children had been admitted to the paediatric ward for observation but all were responding to fluid and electrolyte replacement.

'When do I turn them over?' Tommy asked Jason an hour later as he cooked fish fingers in Jason's apartment. Jason gave him instructions and showed him how to do it with the tongs so he didn't burn his fingers.

Both of their front doors were open, allowing access between the two apartments, with Summer sitting in her living room, trying to sort through the mound of decorations Jason had insisted on purchasing during their mad dash to the shops once they'd left the hospital.

'There's far too much here,' she remarked to herself.

'You can never have too much,' Jason said, and she turned to find him lounging in the doorway, a glass of milk in his hand.

'Where are we going to put them all?'

'Around the apartment.' He held out a hand to her. 'Come. Look at my place.'

She willingly took his hand in hers and headed to his place. 'See? Tinsel strung from the ceiling. Little ornaments on the tree. Stockings hung over the fireplace, which never gets lit because it's a fake fireplace.'

Summer laughed as they made their way back into the kitchen. Her son was standing on a step-stool next to the stove, carefully watching the fish fingers in the frying pan.

'Are they ready now?' he asked Jason.

Jason checked, nodded and then turned to Summer. 'Right. Out. Out you go and sit down at the table.'

'It's all right. I can help.'

'No, Mum,' Tommy told her. 'JD and I are doing the dinner tonight. You get a rest.'

'Oh!' She was touched. Deeply touched, and looked from her son to Jason. 'Well…thank you.'

'You deserve it. Now, go and sit, please.'

She did as she was told, astounded at such personal service. It was true that she'd had servants waiting on her during her entire married life but this was nowhere near the same thing. Tommy was learning different skills and he was learning them under Jason's guidance.

Tommy chattered through their comfortable family-type dinner, telling her exactly how to cook fish fingers. Afterwards, they stacked the dishwasher—still refusing her help—before they returned to Summer's apartment to string the decorations.

At half past nine, Tommy had fallen asleep on the sofa. Summer watched as Jason put a star on top of the Christmas tree before turning on the twinkle lights. She turned off the ceiling light and the room was flooded with a twinkling glow from the tree.

'Perfect,' Jason remarked, and stood back to admire their handiwork. 'See? Isn't this fun?' He looked over at Summer and she could tell by the lilt of his voice that he was smiling.

'It's better than fun. It's *family* fun.'

Jason didn't move. He could hear a hint of regret and pain in her voice, and decided to stay silent, hoping she'd open up a bit more to him.

'My parents died before I met and married Cameron.' The words were soft and had a far-off tinge to them, as though she was talking about someone else. 'When I met him, I thought, Here's my chance to have a family of my own. To be a part of a family again. I wasn't sophisticated. I wasn't polished. I used to wonder what Cameron saw in me. It was like he was the most popular boy in the school and he wanted to go out with me. *Me?* A girl who was only tolerated by the cool kids because her parents made lots of money.'

Jason raised his eyebrows. He'd presumed as much but now it was confirmed. It didn't matter to him. Money wasn't the be-all and end-all of life and Amanda had helped him to learn that lesson. Now, though, he wanted to go to Summer, to hold her while she spoke, to let her know that he was there for her, but at the same time he didn't want her to stop talking.

She laughed without humour. 'I told myself that Cameron must have been interested in me—as a person—because he had heaps of money of his own. With him, I wasn't a target for someone who just liked me for my money.'

She sighed and walked slowly over to the tree. 'The Christmas before my parents died was the last time I had a tree like this. It was the last time I felt like myself—like the *real me*. We didn't have servants. My parents never flaunted their money and they'd worked so hard to achieve all their goals. They used to tell me that anything was possible if I just put my mind to it.' She smiled with a touch of sadness. 'That was how I got myself through medical school. The power of positive thinking. They did good things, my parents, and they were true to themselves. Honest, hard-working people who'd been a lot luckier than others.'

There was that word again. Honest. It had come up time and time again ever since they'd first met. Jason moved now, walking over to place his arm about her. It seemed like the most natural thing in the world to do and equally as natural for Summer to lean into him, resting her head on his shoulder as they stood and watched the tree lights cast their merry glow about the room.

'Thank you,' she said softly.

'You don't have to thank me, Summer. I did it because I wanted to.'

'I'm not thanking you for the tree or the decorations, Jason, although I do appreciate them. I'm thanking you for listening. For letting me talk. For letting me be myself.'

'I haven't *let* you do anything, Summer. You are who you are and it's important that you be that person. I *accept* you for who you are but you do the same thing for me.' He took a deep breath in and knew it was time to tell her more, more about his old life. 'The past couple of years haven't been easy, with the separation and then the divorce. Amanda loved money and power and prestige, too. It didn't matter how much she got, she wanted more. I didn't. Money has never impressed me. It can't buy happiness or love.'

'You mentioned you moved to Melbourne and didn't really see much of each other. Both of you were working?'

'Yes.'

'There's more.' It was a statement.

'Yes,' he answered. 'I guess the long and short of it all is that I wanted children and in the end it turned out that Amanda didn't.'

'She said she wanted them when you first got married?'

He nodded. 'It was all planned. She'd model for a few years, have a child or two and then go back to modelling if she wanted. There was no way I wanted to stand in the way of her dreams but back then I thought we both had the same one. Turned out I was wrong.'

'She got a taste of real success?'

'Exactly.'

'A baby would ruin her figure?'

'Yes.' Jason frowned but there was a slight smile touching his mouth. 'Did you know her?'

Summer chuckled. 'I know a lot of women *like* her. A lot of men, too. Willing to put family and everything else on the back burner, willing to sacrifice the realities of life for their fix of power.'

There was something in the way she spoke that made him realise she spoke from a personal hurt. 'Cameron?'

'Yes.'

'Summer, I'm sorry but I have to ask.' He turned her so she was facing him. 'Why didn't you leave him? It doesn't sound as though your marriage was all that happy. Why did you stay?'

Summer shifted away from his gaze and looked at the sparkling tree again. 'He told me if I made any attempt to leave him, he'd fight for sole custody of Tommy. He said he'd move heaven and earth to take my son away from me.' She shrugged her elegant shoulders. 'I was caught.'

Jason shook his head, hearing her pain at the *thought* of losing Tommy. It was clear that her son meant everything to her and he knew then and there that Summer's words were real. Her actions blended with her behaviour, not only towards her son but towards everyone she met. Where he'd first thought she was an aloof and stand-offish princess, he now realised she was more shy and reserved, playing her cards close to her chest.

Well, she'd trusted him enough to show him those cards, to lay herself open to him, and in turn he respected her for it.

'What about you?'

'What about me?'

'When did you realise you were caught between a rock and a hard place?'

'When Amanda told me she'd been accepted for a show in Europe. I didn't want to go.' He shook his head. 'That surprised me because when we met I thought I would be willing to follow her to the ends of the earth. Turns out I didn't.'

'Where is she now?'

'Milan, darling.' He put on a fake accent and she couldn't help but smile. 'On the catwalks in Milan.'

They stood there in silence for a few more minutes before turning to look at Tommy, who was still sound asleep. 'He's a good kid, Summer. You've done a great job in raising him. The more I know him, the more I like him.'

'My sentiments exactly,' she said, but she wasn't looking at her son when she spoke.

For the next two weeks the hospital was not only hit with Christmas fever but talk of the charity ball to be held at the Ballarat Country Club. Apparently the event consisted of two parties, one for the adults and one for the children. Supervision was provided, activities were planned and, given that it was daylight savings and the sun remained up until almost nine o'clock in the evening, the list of activities for the children was quite extensive.

'Can I go, Mum?' Tommy begged.

'I suppose Bradley's going?'

'And Damo and Mikey. Aw, go on. Say yes.' He turned to Jason. 'JD. Tell her. It's safe. It's monitored. She'll be in the next room and it'll be great.'

'He has a point,' Jason said as he carried in two cups of coffee and placed them on the table before sitting next to Summer. 'We'll be in the ballroom, they'll be down the corridor, and my parents and their childminding staff will be responsible for the children's party.'

'And it's for *charity*, Mum,' Tommy added, as though that was the clincher.

She looked from one to the other. 'Well, as you've both worked so hard on your scripts to convince me this is the right thing to approve, I guess I can't disappoint Brad and Damo and Mikey, so OK. You can go.'

'Yes!' Tommy, her previously quiet and reserved son, punched the air. 'I'm gonna go call the guys and let them know.'

'He never walks anywhere any more,' Summer protested, but smiled as she spoke. She took a sip of her coffee and tucked her legs beneath her on the lounge. Over the last few weeks she and Jason had taken things slowly, spending time with Tommy, enjoying quiet evenings together either at her place or his. Then around ten-thirty, Jason would take his leave, kissing her once on the lips before he left.

The kiss they'd shared in the lift had been powerful, so much so that they both knew things needed to calm down a bit or they'd risk getting carried away too far, too fast.

'I can't do that again,' Jason had explained to her one night. 'I can't rush into a relationship because of an attraction. We need a solid foundation, Summer, and the only way we can get that is to keep spending time together.'

And that was what they'd done. Now it was only two days before the big charity event which would raise money for new equipment in the A and E department. As usual, the event had been sold out about a day after the tickets had been released. There would be raffles and prizes throughout the evening as well as the acceptance of donations from large companies in support of the hospital.

'So. Do you know what you're going to wear?' Jason asked as he watched her, shifting around again so she was comfortable. When she'd first come to town, he doubted whether she would have sat the way she was now. However, slowly but surely, she was letting go of the groomed socialite she'd been forced to become and was getting in touch with the woman who'd been repressed throughout her marriage.

'Wear?'

'To the ball?'

Summer grimaced. 'I don't know. I guess I can find something.'

'No. Actually, that won't do.'

'What?'

'You can't just pull something out of your closet and throw it on for this type of event. This is the highlight of Ballarat's Twelve Weeks of Christmas. It's *the* event of the year and from what I hear, as far as the ladies are concerned, it's all about the dress. Once you have the dress, everything else falls into place.'

'What are you going on about?'

Jason rolled his eyes and shook his head. 'Subtlety was never my strong suit. My sister Cassandra wants to know if you have a dress for the ball because if you don't, she apparently has the perfect one in mind.'

'Oh.' Summer's interest was definitely piqued. 'I forgot that she's a dress designer. Is she coming to the ball?'

'She wouldn't miss it. She'll be here tomorrow and she's asked that you go round to my mother's house for a bit of pre-event pampering and the choosing of the dress.'

'Uh…well… OK, then. I'll go around after work tomorrow.'

'And I'll look after Tommy.'

'Jason, you don't have to.'

'I know. I want to. Besides, we have some camping business to discuss.'

'I'm beginning to doubt that we're ever really going on this camping trip. It's a month today until Christmas. School breaks up in a week's time and then the big day will be rapidly upon us.'

'I've had some strict criteria to adhere to, don't forget.'

Summer reflected. 'Yes, you have.'

'Still, it'll happen. Don't you worry about that.' He tapped the side of his nose and winked at her. 'Leave it all to me.'

When Summer knocked on the door to Jason's parents' house on Friday after work, she wasn't sure what to expect. The door was flung open and female laughter filled the air. Where she'd thought it would just be Jason's sister, it appeared there were a few more ladies around for a bit of pampering.

'Summer. Glad you could make it.' Cassandra embraced her as though they were long-lost friends. 'Come on in. Champagne?'

'Um…all right.' Summer smiled as she saw Alyssa, Rhonda and Mags sitting on chairs in the living room. Dresses in all colours and styles were hung around the room and the discussions as to who should wear what was definitely under way. Elsie, Jason's mother, greeted her just as warmly as her daughter had.

'I'm so glad you could come. Here you are.' She slipped a champagne flute into Summer's hand and led her over to a chair. The other ladies welcomed her, the conversation natural and free. Social gatherings where only ladies were present had played a very big part of her life in Sydney but, again, this wasn't held in a hall or a banquet room. The ladies here didn't automatically size Summer up by what designers she was or wasn't wearing. There were no conversations that started with 'You'll never guess what I heard at the spa the other day' before malicious gossip was revealed with utter glee.

No. These were hard-working ladies, getting together to enjoy themselves and to choose a dress from the brilliant creations Cassandra had made. When they started trying them on, the fun and laughter only started to increase, Summer joining in and having a wonderful time.

'I have the most perfect dress for you,' Cassandra declared, taking Summer's hand. 'I put it in the back bedroom because I didn't want anyone else to have it but you. It's going to knock my brother's socks right off.'

'It is?'

'You're in love with him, right?'

Summer was a little stunned but one look at Cassandra told her the woman practised honesty, just like her brother did. 'Is it that obvious?'

Cassandra laughed. 'Would it bother you if I said yes?'

Summer pondered this and realised that it didn't matter at all. She was certain most of the hospital staff knew how much time she'd been spending with Jason lately and while they didn't

flaunt it at work, it was no doubt clear in the way
they looked at each other.

'You know he feels the same way,'
Cassandra prompted.

'He does?' Summer wasn't so sure. Jason was
cautious, taking things slowly so neither of
them got hurt, but did that mean that he loved
her?

'There's this great saying my parents live by
and they've passed it on to both Jason and me.
"Only the soul that loves is happy." It's by
Goethe.' She pulled a dress still zipped into a
plastic cover out from the closet. 'Jason thought
he'd found love but, sadly, it wasn't to be. And
then…there was you.' Cassandra stopped what
she was doing for an instant and shook her head,
smiling warmly. 'I've never seen him like this
before. He's happy—truly happy—and that's
how I know he's in love with you.'

Before Summer could say a word, Cassandra
took the dress out and held it up. 'Here it is. I
only finished it last night after I arrived.'

'Cassandra.' Summer breathed out with
appreciation as she looked at the strapless
ballgown with multi-layered skirts in a mix-

ture of red, orange and yellow organza. 'It's stunning.'

'Jason said you knew clothes, knew designers, so I'm definitely going to take your reaction as a compliment.'

'You should. It's the most perfect dress I've ever seen.'

Cassandra eyed her creation critically. 'I haven't named it but I think I'm going to call the dress *Summer* because it has all the perfect summer colours in it and it is so completely *you*.'

'I can't carry off all of those bright colours.'

'Oh, yes, you can. Trust me on this. I know what I'm talking about. Now, come on, let's get you into it to see how it looks.'

Summer allowed herself to be persuaded and tried the dress on, loving the way it swished and moved with her. She stood on tiptoe, admiring her reflection.

'See. If we put your hair up with some curls and— Oh, my gosh, I almost forgot the shoes.'

'Shoes?'

'Yes. I guessed last time we met that we were about the same size and I couldn't go past these shoes when I saw them. They're simply perfect for the dress.' Cassandra pulled a shoe box from the closet and put it on the bed. When she lifted the lid, it was to reveal a pair of red pumps.

'They're gorgeous.'

'Oh, yes. Dorothy's ruby slippers have got nothing on these shoes.'

The overall effect was startling and Summer simply stared back at her reflection in total shock. She looked every inch the Sydney social-ite but this time, somehow, her true personality shone through. The colours of the dress were something she would never have chosen for herself but Cassandra was right. It suited her—as did the incredible shoes.

'"Only the soul that loves is happy,"' Summer repeated softly, her eyes radiating hope. She loved Jason, more than she'd loved any man before in her life, and even if he didn't love her back, even if his sister was mistaken and she wasn't as important to Jason as he was to her, she realised that it wouldn't be the end of the world. Of course her life would be miserable but it had been worse before and she'd survived.

She loved him. And because of that, her soul was happy.

Now all she had to do was to make Jason love her the same way, and she'd start at the ball—by showing him the real Summer. The real woman inside this gorgeous gown who he'd help teach to overcome her personal demons and fears.

She was strong, she was intelligent, and she loved the most perfect man on the earth.

CHAPTER TEN

JASON was on his third attempt at tying his bow-tie, the collar of the tuxedo feeling way too tight around his neck. The phone rang and he was glad of the interruption, quickly answering it.

'Jason Daniels,' he said into the receiver, brushing some lint from his trousers.

'Dahling. How are you?'

Jason froze as Amanda's sultry tones floated down the line. 'Fine. How are you, Amanda?'

'Never better. Listen, this is just a quick call to say Merry Christmas. Thought I'd better get in early due to the fact that I'll be in Paris the day before Christmas, in New York on Christmas Day and then the day after I'm off for a well-earned break in Mauritius.'

'OK. Merry Christmas, then.' His first instinct was to hang up the phone but he didn't follow through with it. Her tinkling laughter came down the line and where it had previously always managed to twist his gut and make him want to hold her just one more time, this time it didn't happen. He frowned. 'What are your plans for New Year?'

'There's apparently an excellent party in Madrid so a few of us are thinking of seeing what that would be like, but another part of me is thinking I might go skiing instead. There's nothing like New Year on the slopes. Davos is nice this time of year.'

As he listened to her talk, he realised he wasn't having the same reactions he'd had when she'd called in the past. While she'd hurt him badly, the divorce had been amicable. Now he was starting to realise that perhaps she hadn't really hurt him as much as he'd initially thought or perhaps he was really starting to heal. They'd parted because their lives had been destined to go in two different directions.

Amanda had been right when she'd said he could go with her to Europe, to get a job at a hospital in Milan, but it hadn't been what he'd wanted to do. Why hadn't he? As she continued to try to impress him with stories of the famous people she'd met, Jason began to realise that if he'd really loved Amanda as much as he'd thought, then he *would* have followed her, he *would* have moved heaven and earth to be with her. And he hadn't.

He checked the clock and realised if he didn't get Amanda off the phone and get his bow-tie tied, he'd be late for Summer. Summer. At the thought of her, his heart jumped. Jason stared at his reflection. If Summer told him she was going to leave, to move back to Sydney or shift to Melbourne or New Zealand or France or Germany or the North Pole, he realised he'd follow her. He *would* follow her, and why? Because she was real. She had all the qualities he'd originally thought Amanda had possessed and she had them in abundance.

'Listen, Amanda. I have to go. Tonight's the night of the charity ball and if I don't make a move, I'm going to be late.' He cut her off in mid-sentence.

'Oh, the charity ball. Going stag?'

'No, as a matter of fact, I'm not. Anyway, look, it was great to chat. You take care and don't break a leg on those Davos slopes. *Ciao.*'

With that he hung up, no doubt leaving his ex-wife stunned, but that wasn't his problem any more. Shaking his shoulders, he felt free. Free of his past and anxious to get his future under way.

With his tongue between this teeth as he concentrated, he turned his full attention back to the bow-tie. His future was waiting.

Jason paced around Summer's lounge room, tugging on the bow-tie he'd had eight goes to get perfect. What was taking her so long? He'd been anticipating this moment for so long, especially as he knew she would be wearing one of Cassandra's special dresses.

He'd seen Summer dressed in casual clothes, work clothes, pyjamas, and all of those times she'd exuded elegance and poise. He knew she'd initially been reluctant to go to the charity ball as she'd attended these sorts of functions all the time in Sydney, and dressing up was nothing special to her, as it was for their colleagues. He knew that whatever dress she'd chosen from Cass's creations would look incredible on her and his impatience was starting to take its toll.

'You'll make a hole in the carpet,' Tommy pointed out as he sat there, just as eager to get going as Jason was, but he'd been taught to sit still and remain on his best behaviour. 'At least, that's what Mum says when I used to walk up and down.'

'Hmm?' Jason looked at the boy and only then realised he'd been pacing. He stopped. 'Yes. You're right.' He sat next to Tommy. 'So… looking forward to tonight?'

'Yep. Brad said the country club is awesome and last year there were heaps of activities for the kids from hoops to bowling.'

'Lawn bowls,' Jason corrected with a smile. 'The club is just out of town on a big property. There's a croquet lawn, too, and stables.' At the mention of horses he saw Tommy shift nervously and instantly remembered what Summer had told him. Did Tommy still have a fear of horses? If so, Jason wouldn't blame him, given what he'd been through, but he should also know it was important to work hard at overcoming his fears.

Was that what *he'd* personally been doing ever since he'd met Summer? The woman had driven him wild, tied him up in knots, but he'd known if there was ever going to be anything more than friendship between them, he'd have to overcome his own fears. The possibility of having his heart broken again was definitely a gamble but he'd come to realise that Summer was definitely worth it. He loved her. Just like that, he'd come to realise she meant more to him than any other woman ever had, and it was *that* reasoning which had helped him to take that step out onto the ledge again, to risk his heart. Now all he had to do was convince her that they belonged together—for ever—and tonight was the most perfect night to accomplish it. If she ever finished getting ready, that was.

'There's riding?'

Tommy's words brought Jason back to the present. He put a hand on the boy's shoulder. 'You don't have to do anything you don't want to. OK? You're an intelligent boy and you don't need to prove anything to anyone so don't let anyone goad or coerce you into doing something you're not ready to do.'

'I liked riding. I used to ride every day. My first pony was called Smoky because he was grey.'

'Good name.'

'And then I had Skipper, he was a bit bigger.'

'Well, when you're a growing boy, you need a bigger pony.'

'And then…' Tommy's lip quivered. 'I had Guido.'

'Guido?' Jason smiled. 'Incredible name for a horse.'

'He was my first proper horse.' Tommy hung his head. 'And my last.'

Jason kept his hand on Tommy's shoulder, hoping to reassure him. He'd wanted to have children— No, he *needed* to have children, and this sort of thing, helping them through tough times, was part of it. He already loved Tommy like his own son and he was going to be there for him.

'I'm scared of horses.' The words were only a whisper.

'That's OK,' Jason told him firmly.

'It is?'

'Sure. Your mum's scared of spiders. Some people are scared of snakes. Other people don't like horses either.'

'They don't?'

'They don't, and for all sorts of reasons. You don't need to be ashamed of being afraid of something, Tommy, but also you can't let it hold you back from doing something you like doing.'

'I really did like riding horses.'

'I'm sure you did, and I'll bet you were really good.'

Summer walked into the hallway and was about to announce herself when she saw the two most important men in her life sitting on the lounge, Jason's hand on Tommy's shoulder.

'My dad died.' The words were soft and small and brought an instant lump to Summer's throat. Was this it? Was her son's personal drought ready to break? She held her breath, watching as he looked at Jason.

'He got stood on by a horse. That's why I'm scared.'

'You have a good reason, then.'

Tommy frowned a little. 'My dad wasn't a good dad. He didn't like me. He died before I could make him like me.'

Jason's gut wrenched. 'It wasn't your fault, mate,' he urged. 'Do you know that?'

'But if only I'd been better. If I'd worked harder. He—'

'No.' Jason stopped him. 'It wasn't your fault.' He said each word clearly and slowly. 'Your mum told me what happened, Tommy, and nothing that happened was your fault.'

Summer bit her lip, gripping her hands together, not wanting to make a sound to break this most precious moment.

Tommy processed Jason's words, a look of deep concentration etching his face. 'Are you sure?'

Jason nodded emphatically. 'I'm positive. Dads are supposed to be there for their sons. To help them. To show them how to do things.'

'Like cooking fish fingers?'

'Exactly.' Jason met the boy's eyes. 'Your dad wasn't there for you and that wasn't your fault either.'

'So even if I'd been better…even if I'd worked harder…' He trailed off.

'It wouldn't have changed what happened.' Jason took a deep breath and slowly let it out. 'It's OK to feel bad or sad or upset or even angry at the way things turned out.'

'It is? But I thought I was supposed to be calm

and controlled at all times. That's what my dad and grandfather used to say. Men are controlled. In charge. All the time.'

Jason shook his head, only imagining what the poor young boy had been through during his seven years of life. 'Nope. I'm not like that. Neither is my dad.'

'You're not?'

'I don't think we were too controlled when we were falling over in the big clown shoes, were we?'

Tommy smiled. 'You were so funny.'

'See? Sure, there are some things you have to be serious about and exercise a level of control over, but you don't need to live your entire life like that. If we were like that, we'd end up...I don't know, more like...'

'A robot?'

'Precisely, and we all know robots aren't human.' Jason leaned a little closer as though he was about to reveal an important truth. 'Also, men can cry, Tommy.'

His eyes widened. 'Have you?'

'Yep.'

'But I think you're totally cool.'

'And there you go. Cool men aren't afraid to show their emotions. They're not afraid to say how they feel. They're not afraid to stand up for what they want and they're not afraid to back down when it's needed.'

Then, surprising him yet again, Tommy shifted and wrapped his arms about Jason's neck. 'I wish you were my dad,' he whispered in Jason's ear, and Jason closed his eyes, holding the boy close and wanting the same thing.

When he opened his eyes, he saw Summer standing in the doorway, a trembling hand at her mouth as she watched the two of them with those big blue eyes of hers. She was half-hidden in the shadows and obviously hadn't wanted to disturb them. How long had she been there? How much had she heard?

'Look who's finally ready,' Jason said softly to Tommy, and pointed, unable to take his eyes off the woman he loved. Tommy turned and Jason watched as Summer immediately dropped her hand and pasted on a smile, walking towards them.

'Wow, Mummy. You look really good.'

Jason stood and stared as she came forward into the light. 'Yeah.' It was all he could manage, the power of speech having left him at the sight of her. No one moved, the two of them connecting through the unspoken communication they seemed to have. To say she carried the dress was an understatement. Her hair was up on top of her head with little blond tendrils hanging down here and there. Her eyes were shrouded in a dark blue colour fringed with black lashes which definitely enhanced the sultry look she was giving him now. Her lips were painted with a red-pink lipstick which highlighted their plumpness and simply begged him to kiss her, but the way she was looking at him told him something he'd never expected to see—that she'd dressed up, that she'd wanted to look pretty...*for him.*

Tommy nudged Jason, who was now staring open-mouthed at the woman before him. Classy, Daniels. Real classy. He closed his mouth before swallowing. 'Summer.' When he spoke her name, he wasn't at all surprised to discover his voice was heavily laced with desire. Jason walked slowly towards her, taking in the astounding creation his sister had made and the stunningly beautiful woman wearing it. 'I have never, in my life, seen a more… glorious sight.'

Summer glanced down at the ruby slippers she wore. They made her feel as though anything could happen tonight or perhaps that was Jason and the way he was looking at her. She smiled alluringly at him as he took her hands in his, holding them wide and taking his time to visually caress her body. Summer's breathing started to increase but she worked hard to keep herself under control, especially given that Tommy was in the room.

'You're…' Jason searched his vocabulary but shook his head. 'Not even the word "stunning" can describe how incredibly beautiful you look.'

Summer smiled shyly, loving every compliment he gave her because she knew he meant it. 'Thank you.' She squeezed his hands.

'I mean it. You are going to steal every person's breath when you walk into that room, you know that, don't you?'

'*We're* going to steal their breaths. You look pretty handsome yourself.'

Jason let go of one of her hands and ran his

finger around the collar of his shirt. 'It's a little tight. I never wear it except once a year at the Christmas ball.'

Summer arched an eyebrow. 'Perhaps we can think of another reason for you to wear it.' Her words were suggestive. They were supposed to be, and she saw by the brief flick in Jason's eyes that he hadn't missed her meaning.

'So *now* can we go?' Tommy asked as he walked over to the door, impatience written all over his face.

'Yes, darling. We can. I just need to get my bag.'

Tommy rolled his eyes but waited by the door. 'I'm so glad I didn't have to dress up like you two.' The boy was wearing a pair of jeans with a T-shirt depicting his favourite band. He carried a jacket in his hand which Jason knew Summer was making him take, knowing the evening would turn cool. Running shoes were on Tommy's feet and his hair was slightly spiked up. Even this boy was different from the seven-year-old he'd met not that long ago. He was more relaxed and Jason sincerely hoped that after what they'd been discussing before Summer's appearance, Tommy would start to settle even further.

'Right. Ready,' Summer announced as she picked up her keys. They headed to the door, Jason holding it for her and ensuring the door was locked as they left. He crooked his arm to Summer.

'Milady.'

'Sir.' She slid her hand with its perfectly manicured nails around his arm and looked up into his eyes.

'We are going to have a fantastic night,' he declared.

'I'm loving it already,' she replied as they headed out to the car, where Tommy was once more waiting for them.

The Ballarat Country Club was marvellous.

'This place was built back in the 1860s by a man who struck it rich on the goldfields.'

'Wow.' Summer had been blown away by the decorated ballroom they were currently dancing in. It had high ceilings, ornately decorated with a large chandelier in the centre. There was a Christmas tree to the side and tinsel glittering brightly around the walls. Twinkle lights made the room even more festive and even though it was still quite light outside, the artificial lighting made the atmosphere inside all the more special. 'It's a beautiful place, even down the other end where the children are. I hope Tommy's having a good time.'

'I'm sure he is. You saw the way he greeted his friends.'

'Yes. Yes, I did.'

Jason pulled her a little closer in his arms as they continued to move around the dance floor. He was glad the band had decided to play a slow song because it meant he didn't need to work as hard to find an excuse to hold her close.

He hadn't left her side the entire evening and again it only served to make her feel very special. She'd come to realise that that was Jason's way. Never had a man been more attentive to her in her life, and it just went to prove that she'd chosen the right man to fall in love with. He was wonderful. He was perfect. He was hers. At least, she hoped he was hers.

Shaking her head, she knew tonight was not a night for those types of doubts. She was going to be happy, to show him how much she cared for him and how much she wanted him to feel the same way. Only happy, positive thoughts were allowed tonight. She rested her head on his shoulder and sighed.

'You feel good.' He bent his head and nibbled her earlobe. 'So right in my arms, Summer.'

'Mmm.' Summer closed her eyes, loving the feelings, the sensations he was evoking. They shuffled around the dance floor with other couples and when the song ended Frank from A and E, who was their MC for the night, asked everyone to return to their seats for some more of the evening's festivities.

'All right. We have some door prizes to draw, we have winners to announce from the silent auction held earlier in the evening and we have presentations to make but before we get started, I'd just like to say a special thank you to the Hoyts Company, which is based in Sydney, for their sizeable donation.'

Jason felt Summer go rigid next to him, her smile still plastered perfectly in place. A few people were leaning over to ask if she'd had anything to do with it, given that her surname was Hoyts, but she politely assured them it had nothing to do with her.

'Thanks to them,' Frank was saying, 'we've not only reached our target for the evening but doubled it.' Frank started clapping and everyone joined in.

Summer swallowed over the lump which had instantly come into her throat. Her whole body seemed to be shaking with a mixture of fear and rage, although she knew that outwardly none of this showed. Jason's arm was around her shoulders and he rubbed her arm, obviously picking up on her posture. It was the only thing that helped calm her but at the first non-conspicuous moment in the proceedings when she could excuse herself, she did so.

Jason wasn't far behind her as she walked down the softly carpeted corridor, ignoring the photographs and paintings that hung on the walls as she headed directly for the verandah. As she stepped outside, Summer took a deep breath in and gripped the rail tightly.

'It's all right, Summer. It's just a donation,' Jason reasoned, knowing exactly what had made her become agitated.

She spun around to face him. 'Just a donation? *Just* a donation? No, Jason. It isn't. It's my in-laws' way of saying they know exactly where I am, that they know exactly what I'm doing, and that they're going to take every opportunity to meddle in my life as much as I'll let them.' She shook her head. 'I thought I was free of them and I worked so hard to get here. I made the decision to leave Sydney, to look for a fresh start for Tommy and myself, and they simply took me to court. I won that battle and moved away.'

She turned her back on him, working exceedingly hard at holding back her tears. 'I was so happy here.'

'You talk as though you have to leave?'

'I...I don't know what to do now. They know I'm here. They've obviously been keeping close tabs on me, otherwise how could they have possibly known about the charity ball? How could they have known to make a donation to some hospital they've probably never even heard of? It's a message, Jason. That's how these people work.'

'The money will help the hospital.'

'I'm not denying that. I'm pointing out that everything has a purpose, a meaning, and most times strings attached. Everything is business and this is the Hoyts way of letting me know they haven't let Tommy go.'

Jason touched her then, putting his hands on her shoulders and rubbing gently up and down on her arms. 'They haven't won anything, Summer. You still have custody of Tommy and you're doing an amazing job of raising him. You'll *continue* to do an amazing job as well.'

'How do you know?'

'Because I know you. You're a great mother, and while this donation to the hospital may indeed be some sort of message, why does it matter? Why are you giving them this power over you? Giving them the satisfaction of hurting you?'

Summer frowned and looked up at him. 'What do you mean?'

'You are a strong woman. Haven't you realised that yet? You don't need to worry about what sort of game your in-laws are playing. All you need to worry about is raising your son right. Tommy is a smart, intelligent boy. Qualities he gets from his mother. You said your husband treated Tommy the way he did because he didn't know any different.'

Summer nodded, her tears disappearing as she listened to what Jason had to say.

'Well, you're breaking that cycle. By taking Tommy away from the control of your in-laws, you have the opportunity to make him into an incredible man by giving him the chance to make real and honest friendships. To make mistakes and to learn from them, rather than being punished for them. To find the strength to face his fears. To love with all his heart.'

She sucked in a breath and slowly let it out, her breathing back to normal, her blood pumping at a more sedate rate around her body.

Jason cupped her face in his hands and looked intently into her eyes. 'You're a good mother, Summer. Don't ever doubt that.' He brushed a kiss across her lips. 'Let the Hoyts throw their money around like heavyweights. It doesn't need to mean anything to you except that the hospital will be able to buy the equipment it needs. You have Tommy. You love Tommy and Tommy loves you. *That's* what is important here.'

Summer closed her eyes and put her arms around him. 'Thank you,' she mumbled against his jacket. She took three soothing breaths then pulled back. 'You're so right. The money is just money. It means nothing to me and I'm not going to let them stop me from living the life I want to live.'

'That's my girl.' Jason kissed the top of her head. 'Now…as we're outside, with a dazzling sunset before us, would you care to take a stroll with me?'

'I'd love to.'

Jason shifted so that his arm was about her waist, holding her close. There was a soft breeze blowing, rustling the skirt of Summer's dress with a slight swishing sound. The sky was a mix of reds, oranges and yellows.

'As beautiful as your dress,' Jason commented as they walked to the far end of the verandah, away from the beat of the music. 'But not as beautiful as the woman wearing it.'

She smiled as she rested against the railing, pleased when Jason's arms encircled her waist, drawing her near. 'You say the sweetest things to me, Jason.'

'You deserve them.'

'Do I?'

He shook his head. 'What sort of number did

your husband do on you? Did he only want you for your money?' As he said the words, he watched as Summer glanced away, the truth momentarily visible in her eyes. 'What? But he had the Hoyts wealth behind him.'

'It wasn't enough. Bad mergers happen. Funds get lost. It's always wise to make a good investment.'

'Did you know? I mean, you didn't have an arranged marriage, did you?'

'No. No. It was worse than that. At least in an arranged marriage, I might not have expected my husband to remain faithful, but Cameron took great pains to court me and win me over. I was a blind fool for so long and then…' She stopped and shrugged an elegant shoulder. 'I caught him with another woman. I'd asked him about affairs before but he'd always denied it. Now he couldn't. After that, he didn't even bother to be discreet. I…' She hung her head. 'I thought about leaving him but I was pregnant with Tommy. So I stayed and played the part of the pretty trophy wife and mother, but from the time I caught him with that other woman until his death, he didn't…we didn't…' She shook her head. 'He didn't want me. I wasn't... enough.'

'What? Oh, Summer.' Jason pressed his lips to hers. 'The man was a fool.'

'No. Cameron was a highly intelligent man. He had great business sense and was brilliant at the hospital and—'

'No. I meant he was a fool for not wanting you. Personally, I can't think of anyone but you. I don't want to be with anyone but you. You...you drive me insane with wanting, with needing.' He kissed her again. It was nothing like the other times either. These were no sweet, fluttering kisses, neither were they testing and exploratory. No. This time when he kept kissing her, it was to press his mouth to hers in a way that was highly possessive as well as securely protective. 'He was a fool,' Jason repeated.

'As was your wife.' Summer slid her fingers up his chest, loving the feel of the contours beneath the white dress shirt. The warmth of his neck caused tingles to flood her body as she played with the slightly curling hair at the nape of his neck. 'She may have thought she wanted a life with money, power and prestige, but none of those things can bring you happiness. Take it from me. I know, and honestly, Jason, even though she may have broken your heart, it's definitely made you stronger. It makes you stop and really evaluate what's important in your life and because of your marriage, because of the pain you've been through, you now know what you want from life.'

'I felt like a failure for so long.'

'I understand. I really do, but as you've helped me to realise, we—on a personal level—didn't fail. It was simply marriage to the wrong person that caused the pain.' Summer looked lovingly into his eyes. 'Honestly, though, I don't know how any woman let you go.'

'Summer?' Jason shifted a little so he could see her face more clearly in the slowly fading evening light. 'Saying things like that implies that…' He stopped, wondering if he should go on. What if he scared her away? What if he was about to make the biggest mistake of his life? He wanted her, he needed her, he loved her, but pushing her, confessing his feelings, might make her run as fast as she possibly could in the opposite direction.

'That I'm in love with you?' she finished.

'Well…yeah.'

'That's because I am.' Had she just blown it? Had she pushed too hard, too fast?

His jaw dropped and his eyed widened at her words. 'You're…you're…?'

'In love with you. I have been for some time.' When he still stared at her, obviously stunned, Summer quickly continued. 'I'm not telling you this because I expect anything from you. You're under no obligation or anything and if I'm rushing you, if it's too soon for you to even think about falling in love and you just want to keep dating then that's fine. Honestly. No pressure. It's just that…well…when you love someone, it's always a good idea to let that person know.' She was starting to babble. Even *she* could hear it but she didn't seem able to stop it either. 'Your sister told me something yesterday. She said that only the soul that loves is happy. Well, my soul is happy and I knew I had to tell you how I—'

Her words were cut off as Jason clamped his mouth onto hers. His arms slid around her back, making her feel secure, safe and special. And that's exactly what she was to him. This time his mouth plundered hers, making her realise that everything she'd experienced with him was nothing compared to the emotions he was evoking right now.

Pleasure. Sweet torture. Euphoria. Excitement. That and many more sensations combined to encompass and overwhelm her as he continued to kiss her to the point where she was leaning against him, unable to support herself as her limbs turned to mush.

On and on his mouth seemed to devour her and she was more than happy for it to happen. How was she ever supposed to let him go now? How could he expect her to simply stick to the words she'd just said, that she was more than willing to keep on dating and not worry about taking things to the next level?

'You love me?' Jason pulled back, looked down into her face, his eyes intent on hers.

'Yes. Yes I do.'

His mouth was back on hers but this time he kept it short.

'I take it you don't seem to mind all that much. About my declaration, I mean.' Summer was still leaning against him, but slowly her mind started sending signals around her body and soon she could stand properly again.

'Mind? Do I *mind*? Honey, I've been trying to figure out a way to get you to fall in love with me so I could start convincing you that we belong together.'

'You *wanted* me to fall in love with you?'

Jason smiled brightly and kissed her luscious lips once again. 'My soul is happy, Summer. My soul is happy because of you.'

It took a second for his words to penetrate her hazy mind. 'You love me?' The words were spoken with such astonishment, such surprise that Jason only loved her more.

'You bet I do. I love you so much, Summer Hoyts. I love everything about you. I love your son as though he were my own.'

'You do? Uh…I mean, it's not astonishing that you do because he's such a terrific person, but you really do.' She shook her head. 'Wow.'

'Summer, I hadn't even hoped to declare my feelings tonight as I thought it was too soon, but now that I have and now that you have, too, I can't stop myself from moving on to the next step.'

'*There* you two are.' Alyssa came rushing towards them, panting slightly. 'We've been looking everywhere for you.' There was urgency in her tone and Summer suspected that if the woman hadn't been trained as a nurse, there would also have been a hint of panic.

'What is it?' Jason asked, shifting to face Alyssa, his arms still firmly around Summer.

'It's Tommy.'

'Tommy!' They both spoke in unison, passion switching to parental concern in an instant. Summer's feet were moving, even though she didn't know where she was going.

'What's happened? What is it?' she demanded.

'There's been an accident.' Alyssa opened the door which led to the other end of the country club. 'Tommy's fallen off a horse. He's badly hurt.'

CHAPTER ELEVEN

'A *HORSE*!' Summer's step faltered and her breathing started to increase and it had nothing to do with what she and Jason had just been discussing. 'A…a…*horse*! What was he doing…?' She was almost starting to hyperventilate and Jason stopped walking and immediately made her sit down and put her head between her knees.

'Breathe, Summer. Breathe.' He snapped his head up to look at Alyssa. 'What's the situation? Is anyone with him?'

'Mags and Rhonda are with him. They went out to assess him.'

'Has an ambulance been called?'

'I don't know. All I was told was that he'd been thrown from a horse.'

Jason raked a hand through his hair. Was this all his fault? He tried to think back to the conversation he'd had with Tommy earlier that night. He'd told the boy that it was all right to face his fears. Had Tommy decided to do just that? Confront his fears by getting on a horse? Bile rose in Jason's throat and he hung his own head, hoping it would help to clear his thoughts.

He kept forgetting the child was only seven and most of the time seven-year-olds took everything at face value. He'd treated patients, he'd spoken to parents, he'd helped and guided them, but with all of them he'd had an objectivity which had helped him to see things more clearly. Not so in this case. He loved Tommy, loved him like a son, and therefore he was surprised when emotion seemed to cloud his logical thought processes.

'He's all right, then?' Summer lifted her head, her colour improved but only a little. Adrenaline was starting to kick in and she stood, heading down the corridor to where the children's party was being held. Jason was by her side in an instant, holding her hand, knowing that whatever had happened to Tommy, they were going to deal with it together.

She squeezed his hand. 'I'm glad you're here,'

she whispered, and an overwhelming sense of rightness washed over her. Having Jason here, by her side, knowing that he loved her, that she didn't have to face things alone any more…it was a true miracle. Her Christmas miracle.

As they rushed through the room where the party was being held, the latest band playing on the stereo, the room decorated with tinsel and balloons, Summer took no notice of anything except the door being held open by Jason's mother, pointing the way they should go.

The early evening light made everyone still visible and she could make out Rhonda and Mags leaning over Tommy, who was lying on the ground.

'Tommy?' Her skirts were lifted as she she raced across the grass towards the fenced area where the horses were.

'Mum?'

At the sound of his voice, her heart started to beat again. He was all right. He was coherent and he sounded fine, if a little shaken.

'I'm here,' she called, heading through the gate someone opened for her, Jason still by her side.

'JD?' Tommy asked.

'I'm here, too, champ.' Mags and Rhonda stepped back as Summer and Jason knelt down beside the boy. Summer didn't care about dirt or dust getting onto her dress or over her fancy red shoes.

'Oh, honey. Are you hurt? Anywhere sore?'

Tommy tried to sit up but both of them put a gentle hand on his shoulder. 'Just lie still until we've had a chance to check you over.'

'That's what Mags said.'

'Mags is right.'

'No apparent fractures. He may have been unconscious for less than a minute. No bleeding. No signs of shock. Bruises and scratches are about all I can report,' Mags told both the doctors as Jason ran his hands systematically along Tommy's limbs.

'Everything feels like it's in the right place. How many fingers am I holding up?'

'Two.'

'Correct. How about now?'

'Four.'

'And what's two plus four?' Jason asked.

'Aw…JD. That's easy. It's six. What do you think I am—three years old?'

Summer laughed as she bent down to kiss her son. 'That's my boy. Oh, yes, that's my boy.'

'Mum!' Tommy was a little embarrassed by the attention but Summer could tell that secretly he didn't mind her kisses.

'Let's sit you up. Slowly,' Jason cautioned.

'I'm sorry if I scared you.' Tommy looked down at his hands before meeting his mother's gaze. 'I didn't mean to. I was trying to be brave. Trying to face my fear, like JD said.'

Jason closed his eyes and shook his head. 'I'm going to have to be more clear in what I say,' he mumbled, and looked at Summer. She could see the pain in his eyes and knew he'd been as worried about Tommy as she'd been. Placing a hand on his cheek, she smiled at him.

'It wasn't your fault.'

'A snake came out,' Tommy continued, his eyes wide. 'Slithered right across in front of me when I was riding. That spooked Eiffel and he reared. I didn't know Eiffel was scared of snakes. I just wasn't holding on tight enough. Guess I'm out of practice.'

'Just a little.' Summer shook her head, her body beginning to relax as the crisis passed.

Her breathing was now almost normal although the pain in her heart, the maternal one which was constantly on alert was still pulsing.

'I'm done with horses. I don't want to ever get on one or go near one again,' he declared.

Summer met his blue eyes, which were so like her own. 'Well, we can talk about that another time. How about we get you home and settled in a relaxing bath? You're going to have quite a few aches and pains tomorrow.'

'Or how about we go and check on Eiffel,' Jason said. 'It wasn't his fault after all, and he might be a little shaken up, too.'

Tommy thought about that for a moment. 'Yeah. I guess he would be.' They helped him to his feet and Summer brushed off her dress.

Jason came up behind her and said softly in her ear, 'Do you trust me?'

Summer turned her head slightly, their lips almost touching. His scent was wild and over-powering and it was still a very new sensation for her to be so up close and personal with him in front of other people. 'Yes.'

'Do you trust me with Tommy?'

'Yes.' The answer was given without hesitation.

Jason was astonished. Although he knew she did, it was something else to hear her say it and to hear it in her voice. It was confirmation that she honestly did love him, that it wasn't simply an infatuation. This was the real deal.

'OK, then.' Jason brushed a kiss over her lips, pulled his bow-tie undone and undid the top button on his shirt. Never had he looked more gorgeous. He took Tommy's hand. 'Let's go and check on Eiffel.'

Summer walked back to the fence and went through the gate, knowing instinctively that Jason was going to help Tommy get back on the horse, to *help* him face his fears in the proper way. He was going to support him, to be there for him, and she knew tonight was only the beginning. Tommy was going to find out what it was like to have a man around who honestly cared about him, rather than one who simply brushed him aside.

She watched as Jason encouraged Tommy to stroke Eiffel and after a few minutes he lifted Tommy into the saddle. The horse and rider didn't move and after a moment she watched as Jason effortlessly climbed up behind Tommy, his arms securely around the boy as he held the reins. After another minute or so, Eiffel started moving, slowly at first, just walking around the arena. Summer had had no idea that Jason could ride and it only emphasised that there was still so much she looked forward to finding out about him.

Tommy's friends were watching and they all clapped encouragingly. The noise startled Eiffel for a moment but Jason had control over the animal. They went from a walk to a trot, from a trot to a gentle canter. Then Jason brought Eiffel to a stop and slid from the horse, leaving Tommy up there. He walked to Eiffel's nose, taking the bridle in his hand and led him around. The whole process was taken step by step and she could see Jason talking to Tommy the entire time. It didn't matter what he was saying, for fifteen minutes after they'd gone to check on Eiffel, Tommy was cantering around on his own, Jason standing in the centre of the ring, encouraging him along.

When they finally returned to Summer's side, she came forward and opened her arms to her son. 'I am so proud of you, Tommy.'

'You are?'

'Of course. I've always been proud of you. That was just so brave.'

'It was?' He seemed flabbergasted at the attention he was receiving, not only from his mother but from his friends as well as they came over and patted him on the back and congratulated him.

'Is it OK if I go play for a bit?'

Summer was about to say it was really time to go home when she felt Jason's arm slip around her waist.

'Five minutes,' Jason answered.

'And no running around,' Summer added as they headed inside. The crisis was well and truly over and everyone else went back to their parties. Everyone except for the two people who were more than happy to stay beneath the now starlit sky. The stablehands were taking care of the horses so Jason slipped both arms around Summer's waist and brought her to him.

'Thank you.' He bent his head and kissed her.

'For what? Actually, I guess I shouldn't ask if you're going to give me kisses.'

He smiled. 'You can have as many kisses as you want for as long as you want.'

'Good.'

'But just so you know, I was thanking you for trusting me.' Jason glanced over to where he could see Tommy and his friends. 'He's an incredible boy.'

'Who needs a man in his life. Someone he already trusts and loves.'

'Yeah?'

'Yes. I need that, too. Someone I already trust and love.'

Jason pressed his mouth to hers. 'I love you, Summer. I want to be with you always.'

'I want that, too.'

'So you'll marry me?'

'Try to stop me.'

'That's a yes?'

'That is most definitely a yes.'

She'd expected him to kiss her, to seal the deal, so to speak, but all she got from him was, 'When?'

'When what?'

'When will you marry me?'

'Impatient?'

'Yes. Very.'

'Well, then, I suppose it should be as soon as possible.'

'How about Christmas?'

'A Christmas wedding?' She thought this through. 'At least I can be assured you'd never forget our anniversary.'

His smile was huge, his eyes were smiling. 'A Christmas wedding.'

'Sounds perfect.' She nodded and urged his mouth to her own.

Where Summer had been looking forward to a very different type of Christmas, one to help signify the beginning of her new life, she hadn't ever dreamed that this Christmas would also be the beginning of her life with Jason.

Tommy had been ecstatic at the news that his hero, JD, was about to become his new father and had taken to calling him 'Dad' at every turn. She would often hear him on the phone to Brad or Mike saying things like, 'My dad's taking me camping in the holidays,' or, 'My dad will know. He's really smart. He knows everything.' It warmed her heart to see the two men she loved bonding so completely.

Where the hospital had been abuzz with the Twelve Weeks of Christmas, it appeared the

Christmas wedding was far more fascinating. Cassandra had insisted on making Summer's wedding dress and the Ballarat Country Club had accepted their very late booking for the venue.

Jason had asked Tommy to be his best man and Alyssa and Rhonda were to be Summer's bridesmaids. Jason's father, Brian, had had tears in his eyes when she'd asked him to give her away and everything, somehow, fell neatly into place.

The only tradition she'd bucked was that of an engagement ring. Instead, she'd chosen a wedding band, encircled with diamonds. It was dainty, small and absolutely perfect. It was also a million miles away from the large diamond engagement ring and equally heavy wedding band she'd worn previously. Simplicity was the order of the day and Summer was thrilled when Jason chose a matching gold band with a strip of platinum in the centre of his ring to match her diamonds.

'His and her rings,' he'd remarked.

'Matching. Equal,' she'd replied. 'Now, are you going to tell me where we're going on our honeymoon?'

'I've told you before. It's a surprise.'

'I'm a little concerned, though.'

'About Tommy? He's going to stay at my mum's house for the wedding night and then join us the next day.'

'No. I'm not concerned about Tommy.'

'Then what?'

'Well…you did tell me quite a while ago that you were going to take me camping.'

'And?'

'And we haven't been yet.'

Jason's grin had widened and he'd kissed her. 'Trust me,' was the only answer he was going to give. So Summer had trusted him.

Now she was standing in a small room at the Ballarat Country Club, their friends and family in the ballroom waiting for her arrival. She turned and looked at Jason's mother, the woman who had welcomed her so warmly into the family.

'How do I look?' she asked.

Cassandra stood from fussing with the hem of the dress. Both women stepped back and sighed. The dress was made of cream-coloured raw silk. It was straight, showing off Summer's amazing silhouette. She'd decided against a veil, wanting to see Jason's face clearly while she said her vows. 'Like the most beautiful bride in history,' Elsie remarked. 'My son is a very lucky man.'

Summer shook her head. 'I'm the lucky one. I've been so alone for so long. I know I had Tommy and without him my life would have been desolate, but now I have parents, friends and a talented sister who makes the most amazing dresses.' Summer sniffed and Rhonda quickly stepped in with a tissue.

'Enough of that. Your make-up will run.'

There was a knock at the door and Jason's father, Brian, put his head round. 'Ready? Jason's starting to get impatient and, let me tell you, it takes a lot to make my son impatient.' When he looked at Summer he shook his head. 'And I can see *why* he'd be impatient. You look lovely.'

'Thank you. I think Cass has outdone herself this time.'

'Oh, no,' Cassandra protested. 'The dress may be good but it's the person wearing it who lifts it to perfection.'

'We'd better go and find our seats,' Elsie

said, and kissed Summer's cheek. 'Welcome to the family.'

'Ditto,' Cassandra said, kissing her other cheek. Rhonda stepped forward and made sure there were no lipstick marks on Summer's cheeks.

Brian straightened his own tie and crooked his arm. 'Shall we?'

Summer nodded. 'We shall.'

As Rhonda and Alyssa went before her into the ballroom, the soft sounds of a harp and flute combined to make a romantic melody. Summer took three deep breaths. When the doors finally opened and she saw Jason standing at the other end of the room, Tommy beside him, both looking incredibly handsome in tuxedos, any nerves she'd had disappeared.

The room was decorated with a mixture of Christmas and wedding fare, little white horseshoes tied to the big Christmas tree in the corner. As she walked towards her groom, her step didn't falter. When Brian handed her over to Jason, she felt strong. When the man she loved looked deeply into her eyes, she had not one doubt in her mind that this was the right thing to do.

'Hi,' she said softly.

'I thought you'd never get here,' he whispered, and kissed her cheek. They turned to face the minister and very soon they were making their vows. Vows they'd written themselves, promising to love, honour and cherish each other for ever. They'd included Tommy in the vows as well, her son saying that he accepted JD as his father.

By the time Jason was allowed to kiss his bride, Summer couldn't help smiling when, before he pressed his mouth to hers, he muttered the word, 'Finally.'

The reception was just one big party, everyone in the mood for one enormous Christmas party to celebrate the union of their friends. Eggnog was served along with Christmas pudding for dessert and every time someone tapped the side of their glass with a spoon, Summer and Jason had to kiss. It was the most incredible day of her life, something she made sure she told him as they drove towards the place where Jason had planned their first night together as husband and wife.

They'd said goodbye to Tommy at the country club, looking forward to seeing him tomorrow.

'Where are we going?' she asked as Jason pulled up outside an old-fashioned single-storey house. The large trees in the garden were covered in twinkling lights and the house was ringed with a large verandah, complete with a porch swing. It was old-fashioned, it was comfortable and Summer instantly fell in love with it.

'Somewhere special.' He helped her from the car and walked her up to the front door. He took a key from his pocket and unlocked it before lifting Summer into his arms.

'What are you doing?' She giggled, her arms about his neck, loving the way his body was so close to hers.

'Carrying my wife over the threshold.'

'Threshold?'

'Yes.'

'Aren't you supposed to do that when you've bought a house?' Jason's only answer was to raise an eyebrow at her. Summer stared. 'You bought this house!'

'We can't keep living across the hall from each other.' He kicked the door shut and contin-ued to carry her through the house which had been lit with small battery-operated candles that twinkled prettily.

He finally put her down outside the bedroom door. 'Ready?' he asked.

Summer smiled at him. 'Yes. Ready.' He put his hand on the doorknob but she stopped him. 'Hang on. Ready for what?'

'Your first camping experience.' He opened the door to reveal a large king-sized bed, with rose petals on the floor and scattered slightly over the pillows and sheets but it was what was above and around the bed that made Summer laugh.

'A tent?'

'I remembered your instructions.'

'An honest-to-goodness canvas tent?' she said as she headed into the room. 'You put a tent around the bed?'

'Your instructions were that you'd camp where there was hot running water, a comfortable mattress and a fully functional bathroom.' He pointed to the en suite. 'You also wanted room service. Well, the kitchen is just down the hall.'

'So I did.' She ventured farther into the room, scooping up some of the rose petals and smelling their sweet perfume. 'Smart, wasn't I?'

'Very.' Jason took her in his arms. 'I wanted to make your first camping experience one that you'd never forget.'

'I won't. Believe me. Thank you.' Summer kissed her husband lovingly.

'Because tomorrow, after we pick up Tommy, you'll be enjoying your *second* camping experience.'

'Remember the list. Hot running water. Room service. Bathroom and comfortable mattress,' she dictated, punctuating his mouth with kisses as she spoke.

'Trust me, Mrs Daniels,' he whispered near her ear, and then lifted her into his arms again, carrying her to the bed, desire in his eyes.

Her eyes were alive with love, with laughter and with utter happiness. 'Oh, I do, Mr Daniels. I do.'

MEDICAL™

Large Print

Titles for the next six months…

July

THE GREEK DOCTOR'S NEW-YEAR BABY	Kate Hardy
THE HEART SURGEON'S SECRET CHILD	Meredith Webber
THE MIDWIFE'S LITTLE MIRACLE	Fiona McArthur
THE SINGLE DAD'S NEW-YEAR BRIDE	Amy Andrews
THE WIFE HE'S BEEN WAITING FOR	Dianne Drake
POSH DOC CLAIMS HIS BRIDE	Anne Fraser

August

CHILDREN'S DOCTOR, SOCIETY BRIDE	Joanna Neil
THE HEART SURGEON'S BABY SURPRISE	Meredith Webber
A WIFE FOR THE BABY DOCTOR	Josie Metcalfe
THE ROYAL DOCTOR'S BRIDE	Jessica Matthews
OUTBACK DOCTOR, ENGLISH BRIDE	Leah Martyn
SURGEON BOSS, SURPRISE DAD	Janice Lynn

September

THE CHILDREN'S DOCTOR'S SPECIAL PROPOSAL	Kate Hardy
ENGLISH DOCTOR, ITALIAN BRIDE	Carol Marinelli
THE DOCTOR'S BABY BOMBSHELL	Jennifer Taylor
EMERGENCY: SINGLE DAD, MOTHER NEEDED	Laura Iding
THE DOCTOR CLAIMS HIS BRIDE	Fiona Lowe
ASSIGNMENT: BABY	Lynne Marshall

MILLS & BOON®
Pure reading pleasure™

0609 LP 2P P1 Medical

MEDICAL ™

Large Print

October

A FAMILY FOR HIS TINY TWINS	Josie Metcalfe
ONE NIGHT WITH HER BOSS	Alison Roberts
TOP-NOTCH DOC, OUTBACK BRIDE	Melanie Milburne
A BABY FOR THE VILLAGE DOCTOR	Abigail Gordon
THE MIDWIFE AND THE SINGLE DAD	Gill Sanderson
THE PLAYBOY FIREFIGHTER'S PROPOSAL	Emily Forbes

November

THE SURGEON SHE'S BEEN WAITING FOR	Joanna Neil
THE BABY DOCTOR'S BRIDE	Jessica Matthews
THE MIDWIFE'S NEW-FOUND FAMILY	Fiona McArthur
THE EMERGENCY DOCTOR CLAIMS HIS WIFE	Margaret McDonagh
THE SURGEON'S SPECIAL DELIVERY	Fiona Lowe
A MOTHER FOR HIS TWINS	Lucy Clark

December

THE GREEK BILLIONAIRE'S LOVE-CHILD	Sarah Morgan
GREEK DOCTOR, CINDERELLA BRIDE	Amy Andrews
THE REBEL SURGEON'S PROPOSAL	Margaret McDonagh
TEMPORARY DOCTOR, SURPRISE FATHER	Lynne Marshall
DR VELASCOS' UNEXPECTED BABY	Dianne Drake
FALLING FOR HER MEDITERRANEAN BOSS	Anne Fraser

MILLS & BOON ®

Pure reading pleasure™

0609 LP 2P P2 Medical

1	26	51	76	101	126	151	176	201	355
2	27	52	77	102	127	152	177	202	357
3	28	53	78	103	128	153	178	203	363
4	29	54	79	104	129	154	179	204	375
5	30	55	80	105	130	155	180	205	380
6	31	56	81	106	131	156	181	206	383
7	32	57	82	107	132	157	182	208	400
8	33	58	83	108	133	158	183	212	451
9	34	59	84	109	134	159	184	227	453
10	35	60	85	110	135	160	185	233	460
11	36	61	86	111	136	161	186	234	461
12	37	62	87	112	137	162	187	237	478
13	38	63	88	113	138	163	188	238	486
14	39	64	89	114	139	164	189	241	488
15	40	65	90	115	140	165	190	242	509
16	41	66	91	116	141	166	191	243	511
17	42	67	92	117	142	167	192	262	519
18	43	68	93	118	143	168	193	269	523
19	44	69	94	119	144	169	194	279	534
20	45	70	95	120	145	170	195	288	552
21	46	71	96	121	146	171	196	299	570
22	47	72	97	122	147	172	197	310	575
23	48	73	98	123	148	173	198	312	583
24	49	74	99	124	149	174	199	331	619
25	50	75	100	125	150	175	200	341	624